'The title of his collection of stories is exact: for although his subjects lend themselves to devastating ridicule, he is too good a writer to be content with mere demolition work. He has the rarest of the satirist's gifts — that of using mockery to build character and to express compassion... His sympathy goes to weak, likeable people struggling to keep in step with the demands of social convention: it is against these ... that he directs his most savage comedy.'

*Times Literary Supplement*

'(the title story) is superb, moving, intriguing ... Ustinov, with perfect timing and detail, has here written a great short story, and from this point his book does not falter.'

*Daily Express*

Also by Peter Ustinov in Panther Books
*Krumnagel*

Peter Ustinov

# Add a Dash of Pity

Panther

Granada Publishing Limited
Published in 1976 by Panther Books Ltd
Frogmore, St Albans, Herts AL2 2NF
Reprinted 1977

First published in Great Britain by William
Heinemann Ltd 1959
Copyright © 1958, 1959 by PAVOR SA
Made and printed in Great Britain by
Hazell Watson & Viney Ltd
Aylesbury, Bucks
Set in Linotype Times

# CONTENTS

# THE MAN WHO TOOK IT EASY

Erhardt Von Csumlay was dressed in black, not because his wife had recently died but because black is a serious colour. He watched a smartly dressed crowd streaming into the auditorium of the University of California, and cursed Stravinsky. That fellow had got away with murder. Nothing admirable about him except that he had stuck to his guns. Full marks for tenacity, for belief in himself. But as for talent? What did those minked and sabled ladies know of music? Stravinsky was just a great name for a composer, exotic but not too difficult to pronounce. It looked good on a programme. Like Picasso, there's another one. Catchy. Easy to remember. Von Csumlay was exotic, all right, but too authentic to be popular, too true to itself.

The concert was about to begin. Dr Von Csumlay did not deign to enter. Had Stravinsky appeared in person, his arms outstretched, and said, 'Erhardt Von Csumlay, at last we meet, your passacaglia for strings, two trombones, and percussion has always been the greatest inspiration to me,' Erhardt would have turned away sourly and said, 'I wish I could say the same for a single bar of your music, Herr Stravinsky.' But Stravinsky did not appear. At the time he was in Venice, conducting a new work of his at the festival.

As the first notes of the *Sacre du Printemps* were heard faintly from the interior of the hall, Dr Von Csumlay turned away his head and winced. Then he walked off into the balmy night, searching the past for consolation. He remembered his youth in Hungary, how his grandfather had given him his first undersized violin and taught him the tunes of his native soil. His father had been a professor of music at Nyíregyháza, underpaid and deservedly so. Whereas his grandfather had been an out-and-out peasant, a simple jolly soul with an agreeable smell of toil about him, his father had tried to better himself by glorifying all that was German and academic.

Erhardt remembered him as a small man, prematurely bald, immaculately dressed as a bank manager, his dull eyes staring arrogantly behind a mean pair of pince-nez. He had seemed determined to prove that music was a reputable profession, fit for gentlemen, which had rules as inflexible as the rules of science. As Erhardt practised the violin, for which he had talent, his father would stand by, counting like a human metronome, cane in hand ready to rap Erhardt's fingers at every false note. There were no feelings to the man, just a conviction of what was right and what was wrong. Anything contemporary was automatically wrong.

The boy, who loved music, revolted both against the colourless professionalism of his father and against the gormless spontaneity of his grandfather. At the end of World War I, a new spirit swept across the arts, a spirit chaotic, iconoclastic, and mechanical. God was unseated from the celestial throne by the accumulated bitterness of the defeated, and the man-made machine set up in His place. Melody was displaced by rhythm; beauty by freakishness.

Young Erhardt embraced the new creed with fervour. It spelled liberation from all academic responsibilities, from all the rigidity of which his father was so proud. He grew his hair very long, wore the expression of revolt permanently on his face, and set up house in a Budapest garret with a very dirty Romanian lady twice his age, who believed he could do no wrong.

He caroused all night, talking black philosophy to his

cronies while his mistress smoked knowingly from an immense cigarette holder, and during the day he wrote violent, formless, cruel music, occasionally making love as violent and as formless as his composition. His sonata for three drums was an immediate success and had the honour to be hissed at the annual meeting of the International Society for Contemporary Music. The news of this fiasco d'estime spread far and wide, and he was asked to lecture in America, which he did, marrying the Romanian lady for the sake of American morality. His symphonic poem, *Test Bench,* dedicated to the city of Cleveland, was hissed in that city, and the first performance of his opera for a single voice, accompanied by a double orchestra and a chorus of masked dancers, entitled *Formula 21,* caused a riot at the Metropolitan before the end of the first act. His appearance in Paris unleashed an equal furore. Here he divorced the Romanian lady for the sake of Parisian morality, although they continued living together, and the world première of his concerto for musical saw and nine woodwinds caused a duel between two cabinet ministers, in the course of which one was seriously wounded.

Gradually the world calmed down, and certain of the leaders in the musical world were stealthily reintroducing melody into their words again. Slowly, booing lost its interest for the intellectuals, and applause began to gain ground as a standard of appreciation. Erhardt found it more and more difficult to place his works, and the Romanian lady, with barometric instinct, left him and went to live with a young painter who was making a name for the subtlety of his compositions and the gentleness of his colours.

Erhardt was still a young man, and yet music critics, on those rare occasions on which they mentioned him, attached him so firmly to the very early twenties that he might as well have been dead. Listlessly he remembered the painful interview with his publisher in Vienna. The publisher had asked him to lunch, but changed the invitation to a quick drink, owing to the pressure of business. A bad sign.

'Believe me, it isn't that you are without talent but that you have a deficient critical faculty,' the old man had said, glancing at his watch. 'I am a publisher, not an artist. It is my job to keep my ear to the ground. When the war ended and the Austro-Hungarian Empire had disintegrated, we were all so bewildered that we went wild, and we followed the noisiest leaders, not the best. Cacophony was a valid expression of our desire to destroy, to plunge ourselves into mediocrity, to say to the pleasant, green, Schubertian world the words of the villain of the melodrama, "If I can't have her, nobody shall." But all that has changed now, Herr Csumlay.' The publisher always left out the 'Von' as though he knew it had been added gratuitously by Erhardt himself.

'What do you want me to do?' he had asked the publisher rather foolishly, and he wanted to kick himself now when he remembered it.

The publisher had laughed sourly and said, 'Why ask me? You are the artist, not me. If you feel compelled to go on writing as you have been writing, then go to another house that may be more tolerant towards outworn shock tactics. If, on the other hand, you decide, or are able, to write more maturely, then submit your stuff to us by all means. But let me tell you this, my young friend: the only music worth publishing, apart from salon pieces, is music produced by compulsion, by an inner urge, and even if the result is unpleasant, it is inevitable. Your music is never inevitable. We discern a desire to shock, and it repels us. Take my advice: if there is no force within you which tells you how to write, try salon music, simple tunes which spinsters can play and which may even reach the restaurants. After all, that is music too, and it invariably pays more than the serious sonatas. Think it over. Forgive me for leaving you, but I have an appointment.' And the publisher had left the furious, humiliated Erhardt to finish his beer alone.

Now, as Erhardt walked the unlit street, listening to the summer cicadas and taking in the flickering red halo over Los Angeles, where the neon signs drummed their nervous fingers on the tranquil sky, he thought about that inner urge. So much time had passed that he could now look the publisher square in the eye and dispassionately recollect the criticism levelled at him. After all, what is music? It is a part of nature, a translation of nature with other terms.

The great romantics would have turned the majestic panorama into a splendid, turgid tone poem, evoking by quite conventional means the warm mystery of an August night, with its voluptuous orgy of stars, scattered in profusion over the heavens. Emphasis on the cellos, with some muted brass for a timeless quality. Occasionally a single violin might dislodge itself from the symphonic soup and wander selfishly over the high register, evoking the emotions of the poet, alone with his world.

But what would the romantics have done with the neon-signed, the stuttering, multi-coloured manifestations of restlessness and fever over on the horizon? Had they the equipment to write about what man has done with nature? No, they were only at home with nature itself, with tempests, not with traffic. It would be unreal to be a romantic today.

And yet, had he not perhaps erred by expressing only the sleazy aspects of civilization? He had written only of smoky caverns, of metal structures, of cement and electric light. Outside, in the open, there still were trees, grass, water, the same phenomena which had sparked Beethoven in his Boy Scout hike in the hackneyed Sixth and Mendelssohn in his Cook's tour in the Scottish and the Italian Symphonies. Ah, if only he had lived in the nineteenth century, he could have known real success! He was good-looking, better looking than Liszt. His white hair and anguished brow, his blue eyes, tortured enough to be interesting, would have made the ladies swoon in those ample days of facile emotions and diabolical virtuosi. He could have written a splendid Hungarian Symphony, with each movement carefully named after a recognizable Magyar mood. In his mind, he could read the programme notes. A slow opening movement, 'Moonlight on the Puozta', leads without break into the tumultuous 'Hungarian Village Wedding', and from these the work broadens into the glorious 'Lullaby to a Transylvanian Baby', ending with controlled abandon in a 'Symphonic Czardas' of incredible technical accomplishment. And the violin works! Humoresque upon humoresque, elves' dances without end.

But it was not to be. Here he was, in Los Angeles, in the middle of the twentieth century, faced with both town and country, and without an inner urge to call his own. Just then a police car drove up. It had been following him at a snail's pace for ten minutes.

'Where you heading, Mac?' asked the policeman at the wheel. Walking in Los Angeles is tantamount to loitering.

'I am going to a restaurant,' answered Erhardt, who knew better than to be annoyed.

'Mind telling me which one?'

'Antal Laszlo's Rhapsody Room.'

'Car broken down?'

'I don't have a car.'

'You don't have a car!'

The policeman's face hardened, and he braked. This certainly was suspicious. 'What's your name?' he rapped.

'Professor Erhardt Von Csumlay.'

'Engaged in atomic work?'

'Music.'

'Music? D'you know Perry Como?'

'No.'

'You're a music professor, and you don't know Perry Como?'

The policeman was more suspicious than ever. 'Where d'you work?' he asked.

'Warner Brothers.'

'Warner Brothers? You a movie composer?'

'I am a serious composer, engaged occasionally in writing music for motion pictures.'

'What's your name again?'

'Erhardt Von Csumlay.'

'When I see a name on the screen I can't pronounce, I'll know you wrote the music.'

Erhardt tried to smile.

'What's that restaurant again?'

'Antal Laszlo's Rhapsody Room.'

'Know how to get there?'

'Yes.'

'O.K. Take it easy.'

The policeman drove slowly into the night.

Erhardt detested encounters with officials, but was never surprised or even outraged by them. Europeans had become used to persecution and endless delays on frontiers, and in the process they had learned to talk themselves out of trouble without blushing.

When Erhardt had said that he worked for the Warner Brothers Film Company, it was not quite true. What had actually occurred was that round about 1930, when he was living in Paris, teaching, he had gone to a Montmartre café

one night to drink away his sorrows, when he had heard
Hungarian spoken at the next table. Listening carefully, he
gathered that the party of two men and two women con-
sisted of a film producer, Geza de Amrassy, and a film
director, Lajos Dubay, and that the ladies had no permanent connection with the gentlemen. They were at the sentimental stage of inebriation, and gradually, as coherent
conversation petered out, they began to sing the popular
hits of their youth with clouded passion.

Erhardt wandered to the upright piano, temporarily
abandoned by the resident pianist, and began to hammer
out the old tunes, carrying the moribund voices of the four
Hungarians on the drooping wings of the yellowed notes
into their chosen Elysium. After a while, names and
addresses were exchanged, and soon Erhardt found himself writing the music for a German-language film based
on the life of Lajos Kossuth, the liberator of Hungary. It
was a musical, and Kossuth sang Hungary to freedom in a
somewhat frivolous fashion. Erhardt's success was immediate. He even had an affair with one of the ladies at
the table. More films followed. A musical about Elizabeth
and Essex, and a gay piece about Rasputin entitled *The
Devil's Monk*.

It was inevitable that sooner or later the talented Geza
de Amrassy would be summoned to Hollywood, where he
was known as Gaylord de Race. It was also inevitable that,
when faced with producing a Biblical outburst based on
Judith and Holofernes, a subject for which he had no
aptitude whatever, he would send for Erhardt simply in
order to have someone to talk to. All of Erhardt's facility
for the ear-catching emotional trick was brought into play,
and the high executives raved about his music for *That
Judith Woman*, telling him confidentially that without the
tunes the film would have been a dead loss.

Other movies followed without intermission, with sub-

jects as diverse as jail breaks from Alcatraz and sexy
follies in the court of Ivan the Terrible, erotic encounters
in the Sahara and the escapades of a ninety-foot orang-
utang which threatened the known world. His life took on
a new and successful rhythm. He built himself a house in
a curious Mexican-Gothic style, constructed a pool,
married a starlet, and worked in a room imitated from one
he had seen in Pompeii, his desk surrounded by a shallow
moat of water set with sparkling blue mosaic, which
proved an attractive background for the goldfish. The front
door, which came from a ruined Hebridean castle, was
flanked by a bust of Franz Liszt on one side and one of
himself on the other.

He used to sit at his desk, the waves of light from the
miniature moat reflecting on his forehead, and write every
kind of music to order. He dressed in what he liked to call
his 'creation robe', fashioned in black velvet, with some
Hussar motives worked on it in white cord. Occasionally
he would stride over to a cream-coloured piano and
dreamily strum a few arpeggios. Lazily the borzois on the
sheep-skin rugs would lift an ear and then continue their
picturesque activity of staring at nothing with the distinguished application of duchesses at a charity concert.
He no longer thought in terms of music, but in terms of
remuneration, cards, cocktails, and grandeur. His friendship with Gaylord de Race matured into a complicity.
They would always play poker together, get drunk together, deceive their wives together, and the Marmon
limousine of one was rarely seen without the Pierce-Arrow
convertible of the other parked alongside it.

Mabel Von Csumlay had been a show girl. She was a
platinum blonde, button-nosed, and foolish. The borzois
accepted her as one of them. Occasionally Erhardt would
make love to her, calling her 'my violin, the one on whom
I play my most exquisite melodies of love', and then see

through his half-closed eyes her ecstatic face artlessly posed on its pink pillow, her mouth ajar to receive his kisses, her eyelids closed to contain her poverty-stricken heaven. Aside from these activities, in which he was an expert, more rational conversation was an impossibility. She was furniture, an inanimate object on which to hang jewellery as toys are hung on a Christmas tree.

Life continued comfortably enough until 1941, when without warning one November morning Gaylord de Race dropped dead at his desk during a casting conference. Erhardt had known de Race so well that he suddenly discovered that he knew practically nobody else. The chief of production called him in, and after some conventionally morose reflections about the great guy who had just passed to some greater studio, Erhardt was assigned to an anti-Nazi picture directed by a German expatriate who wore an Iron Cross from World War I on his shirt while at work.

Werner Plack was much more particular in his methods than de Race had been. He worked with his nerves rather than with his head. Erhardt wrote his incidental music with the same abandon that he had always done. To suggest the menace of the approaching Gauleiter, he orchestrated the *Horst Wessel* song in an acidulated manner, while the background to the clandestine gatherings of the French underground movement was but *Frère Jacques* scored for tin whistle and side-drum.

When Plack heard the music, he grew mad with anger. 'All has been done before!' he ranted. 'Without inspiration, without imagination, without stomach!' To the production chief he added, 'How can a Hungarian understand the inner strength of the Resistance heroes and the demoniac sadism of the Nazis? All he does is to take the most obvious elements and dramatize them in the most old-fashioned way.'

'Old-fashioned' is the word most calculated to frighten even the most old-fashioned executive, and so Erhardt was removed from the picture and given a Western to do. He had never done one before, since de Race had concentrated almost exclusively on Easterns. His attempt was not successful. The director growled, 'What the hell's that waltz doing in there?' And it was enough. Erhardt was removed again, and soon his contract lapsed and was not renewed.

All the same, he was sufficiently important not to drop out of sight right away. His noble chords in the various Biblical epics still reverberated in the minds of those old enough to regret the passing of greater days. For a time he did quite well as a climax consultant. He was no longer considered as a composer of full-length scores, but individual producers with climax problems would send for him and say, for instance:

'Professor, we have a scene here which is the climax of the picture, both pictorially and emotionally. The battle of Rappahannock is reaching its closing stages, see? The hero, Brick Johnston, is wounded. His buddy, Red Gogarty, is dead; around him all is death and devastation. Here we superimpose the vision he has of Marilyn Fry, a Southern girl, his sweetheart, in her crinolines. What he sees and what we see is a vision of enduring sweetness, of undying loveliness, of hope and beauty. Do I make myself clear? All his life, he's been a rough-talking, rugged guy with no belief in anything but his own guts and spunk, but now, faced with this vision – the picture's in colour, incidentally – he finds a personal faith, which leads him automatically to prayer. He prays, "Make me worthy of all this loveliness, and please, God, let Marilyn be there, waiting for me, just the way I see her now, when all this killing's over. I want her so badly, and I want her to want me. Please." He prays that way because he's a rugged guy like I said and because he don't know any better. Now here's the melody which we have for the battle scenes, and here's the love tune. What we want is three minutes of real powerful emotional climax music blending the two themes in a triumphant, tragic, yet hopeful, inspirational surge which says to us, "Yes, life's grim and tough at times, but there's always tomorrow, and every cloud has a silver lining." Think you can do it?'

Erhardt would take the bits of paper home and compose some neurotic symphonic fudge in whatever key was indicated. The producers were always satisfied, since, although he was discredited as a writer of sustained scores – 'Too old-fashioned', 'Typical Viennese *Schmaltz*' – he had become an expert on effective climaxes, the only expert, as though he were a surgeon who specialized in only one rare disease, a consultant.

Naturally his life could no longer be conducted on the lavish scale to which he had been used. The house was sold, and Mabel had the first of a series of nervous breakdowns. Her only gift was to be kept, and she had never realized that there was an existence which had to be budgeted. Erhardt moved into a large apartment house, keeping only the cream-coloured piano out of all the luxury. He did his work without regrets. Central Europeans are resilient. They have had to be so often.

One day, he was offered a picture all his own by a small independent company. It wasn't much, an outer-space fantasy about an invasion of astral gnats, but to Erhardt this was like a return to dignity. He was older now, some of the old facility had gone, but he strained every nerve to make this score a thing of power, or urgency, which would mark his return into the tight ranks of the accepted. The theme of the gathering gnat army was eerie enough, and he polished it as though it were a priceless jewel, until every note contributed towards the general architecture of terror. The song of the young lovers, the last inhabitants to be left alive in a world laid waste by the insects, was a tremulous and touching andante cantabile, scored for a mass of strings. The producers were satisfied.

Unfortunately, when the film appeared, two other composers sued the company, the one claiming that the theme of the gathering gnats was stolen *in toto* from his music to a television series about cattle rustlers in Texas, while the other maintained that the song of the young lovers was nothing but a bald paraphrase of a popular number he had composed for a celebrated crooner several years back, entitled *Love Me, Gaucho*. The lawyer for the defence tried bravely to prove that Brahms had once used a theme very much like that of the gathering gnats in a string quartet and that *Love Me, Gaucho* was very reminiscent of a violin piece by Sarasate, played slowly, but both plaintiffs won their cases, and Erhardt was finally and irrevocably finished, through.

He thought back on all that with a little bitterness now. He had not consciously stolen those melodies, but he was over sixty and had heard so much music in his time. Watch enough television and some of the fragments, even of the advertising jingles, are bound to become embedded in the subconscious. Perhaps a composer should live in isolation, never listen to a note of anyone else's music.

'Hey, Professor!'

It was that damned cop again.

'If you want the Rhapsody Room, you should have taken a right two blocks back.'

Why can't he mind his own business?

'Thank you very much.'

'Take it easy now.'

Erhardt retraced his steps. What had he done with his life? He had never been able to choose between high art and commerce. There was no level on which he could even judge himself. Certainly, if by inner compulsion the old publisher had meant the willingness to starve in an attic for the sake of an avant-garde sonata, then he had none. Life is to be enjoyed, and to pretend that any piece of music is worth the sacrifice of its enjoyment is ludicrous. Basically, Beethoven was a fool. A few more schottisches and a few less symphonies, and he could have lived more comfortably, even have gone to the expense of an ear-trumpet perhaps. Was he here to enjoy the glory? Did he get the royalties from his record sales?

And yet, why did Mabel jump from a sixteenth-storey window? What had made her do such a rash thing? It was too late to guess now. He had hardly known her, since there wasn't really much to know. Perhaps there was? Could it have been a deficiency in his character which had frustrated her desire to give more of herself to the man of her choice? Was her incredible dumbness but a mask for a great timidity? He shuddered at the thought, and then, as he had done all his life, he gave himself the benefit of the doubt. Right from the beginning she had been latently hysterical, a child of her times. Women from the new world were different. They had none of the intellectual hocus-pocus which his first wife, the lady from Bucharest, had used in order to give love its savage flavour. But then while the Romanian was fine as a muse for advanced chamber music, she would have been hell in Hollywood. How Gaylord de Race would have hated her! He laughed aloud.

What are women, after all? Transitory comforts. But why had he no children, as his father had, yes, even his stupid father, and his grandfather, and so on, ad infinitum, back to Adam? Why did thousands of centuries of untroubled procreation have to end with him? He lived for love. He wasn't a recluse or a deviate, but for some reason there was no family, no responsibility.

Erhardt thought deeply as he walked, and found no answer. Then it occurred to him that perhaps he had never really matured, that that was the reason he had always seized whatever was available, like a baby, and played with it cruelly and dropped it to see if it would break. He had loved women, but had always foreseen with displeasure that difficult moment when an affair was over, and had spoiled his pleasure even before he had attempted to enjoy it. He had invariably thought, and said, more or less wittily, that life was imperfect and therefore it must be lived to the full. Champagne must flow to drown the sorrows. But how superficial his sorrows were! Now poor Mabel had jumped from the sixteenth floor, and he really felt no great emotion, because he wasn't trained to. He hadn't known her. She had never penetrated.

By rights, he felt, he ought to be crying, and yet there was no trace of a tear. His face was white and very handsome, and all he could do was to sigh mechanically.

Perhaps he had no soul? Too much talent, and no soul. Certainly his early music was not beautiful, but surely it had something? It had inspired audiences to fury, and that was a valid mark in its favour. It could never be accused of being cold or lifeless. His later works had their value too, and they had not been entirely unsuccessful. They had afforded him a splendid house, a pool, some borzois, and a nomination for an Oscar. Incredible what people do with money. Who, in his right mind, wants borzois? All they do is sit around and eat enormous quantities of meat. He smiled. He was giving himself the benefit of the doubt again and sticking to his happier memories.

'Thought you'd never get here, Professor.'

Now that infernal policeman was parked right in front of Antal Laszlo's Rhapsody Room and grinning in an

atrociously friendly way. Probably there was a seasonal dip
in the crime wave. Since there was a scarcity of juvenile de-
linquents, he had to pick on an old man who wished to remember what fresh air was like.

'Food good in there?'

'Excellent. I always come here.'

'Take it easy.'

Erhardt entered the restaurant, and the look on the face
of the hat-check girl was far from reassuring. He kissed her
hand gallantly and passed among the diners, furtively finding his way to a wooden door in the body of the hall,
through which he passed. He was now in a small and cheer-
less room. With nervous fingers he searched for a key in his
pocket, found it, and opened a locker.

Just then Antal Laszlo entered in the uniform of a Hungarian landowner of the last century. He was the proprietor
of the establishment, and the nearest he had ever been to
Hungary was Pittsburg. For the purposes of trade he had
learned the Hungarian words for 'Welcome', 'This way
please', and 'Come again', but for the moment he was too
angry to speak anything but English.

'This is the last break I'm giving you, Csumlay, and I
mean it. If you're late again, you're fired. I'd fire you here
and now if I didn't know you'd just suffered a great personal tragedy. I'm a kindhearted man, but there's limits
and, boy, you've just about reached them.'

Erhardt stammered an apology in servile tones and
changed clumsily into gypsy costume. Taking his violin, he
re-entered the restaurant and mounted the podium. The
other musicians looked at him without expression. He
wiped the perspiration from his brow and glanced over at
the hat-check girl, who was now smiling. Attractive she
was, with her long legs in net stockings, her low décolleté
and her cheeky uhlan shako in royal purple. He gazed at
her with nostalgia. Perhaps she was the woman for this

phase in his career, one who could be thrilled by the hysterical trilling of a gypsy violin? He smiled back, sadly, with distinction. She settled like a cat before the fire, to listen, her pretty face resting on her hands.

The scimbalom cascaded down its full register, and the Hungarian medley was on. Closing his eyes rapturously, and investing his face with the bitter-sweet expression demanded of it by tradition, Erhardt began to play.

A far cry this, from the experiments with the International Society for Contemporary Music, or indeed from the gala premières at Grauman's Chinese, but the hat-check girl was listening, and he was playing beneath her balcony. The diners went on talking doggedly throughout his recital, even raising their voices in order to keep their conversation alive above the folklore, but Erhardt didn't really care. Suddenly the orchestra stopped. This was the cue for him to embark on *Schön Rosmarin* as a solo. Yes, perhaps his early music was trash, perhaps his moving-picture scores were an arrant prostitution of a talent meant for finer things, but here he was, throwing his all into the interpretation of a salon piece by another composer, in a restaurant in which the goulash was inedible. He had not surrendered. Perhaps he had even found his level. Nobody could accuse him of quitting. The diners could go on talking if they wished, it's a free country, but nobody could prevent him from earning his living by music. What he was doing was perhaps not all he had hoped for, but it was something, it was something.

He opened one eye as he played. The hat-check girl was listening with her brows knitted in concentration, her hands joined as though in prayer.

Something? It was more than something. It was art. Valid art. 'But all the same,' he thought, 'curse Stravinsky.'

# THE WINGLESS ICARUS

Everyone at the Writers' Union was surprised at the extent of Comrade Zotin's applause when the novelist, Efim Grigovievitch Grigalka, saw fit to compare Pasternak to a hyena; everyone but the historian, Zasyadko. Grigalka who had some juicy phrases coming about the accursed Pasternak, all of them culled from the world of farm and wildlife to form the kind of agrarian invective which any village idiot could understand, interrupted his diatribe to study Zotin, who was still clapping energetically when all the others had stopped. Could this be a form of irony?

Grigalka's pince-nez glinted as the lenses caught the lights from the chandelier, and the sudden coming and going of those fierce little bulbs seemed to accentuate his annoyance. The faces of the other great writers of the Soviet Union were all turned towards Zotin, expressing puzzlement rather than enthusiasm. 'Sit down,' hissed Zasyadko.

Zotin realized that he may have overdone his eagerness, and so tried to leave a right-minded aftertaste to his demonstration by shouting, 'What you have said is true, Comrade, a thousand times true.' Then he sat down in silence. He glanced at Zasyadko. The two had known each other since 1911. Zasyadko looked at him with the quiet pity of a man who is slow to pass judgment. Zotin blushed slightly, and then craned to listen to some more choice rural similes as the celebrated Grigalka continued to work on the absent Pasternak.

Zasyadko knew what was coming. When Grigalka spoke, it was always the same. It was always the same when Grigalka wrote, and he wrote often and profitably, about cement, about pipelines, about power stations and hydroelectric plants. Every time he opened his mouth, it seemed to Zasyadko that it disgorged a stream of verbal cement. The historian stared at the ceiling and began to daydream.

He remembered Zotin as a young man, a misfit, a man in love with an illusive mistress, literature, who would court her till the end, never admitting defeat. Zasyadko had married young and happily, and like so many serene uncomplicated couples, he and his wife found they were practically forced to adopt the unhappy Arkady Petrovitch Zotin and regarded sheltering him as a kind of debt to pay destiny for their own concord. Even when young, Zotin cultivated the tousled air of rebellion, the pointed beard of the æsthete, and the bad teeth of one whose thoughts are too elevated to stoop to toothpaste. He published a slim volume of futurist poetry in 1913 and cherished a letter of encouragement from Mayakovsky, who was one of the few people to have read it. He spent his time arguing in cellars and in attics, but was rarely seen in the rooms in between. Zasyadko had private means, and he smilingly supported his freakish friend, who attacked all opposition as a terrier attacks a bone.

In 1914, Zotin enjoyed a moment of notoriety when he was arrested by the Czarist police for allegedly writing a scurrilous pamphlet attacking the autocracy. He was released a week later when, with the characteristic zeal of the inefficient, the police discovered that the culprit was another author of the same name. Still, Zotin did not regret this error, since it gave him an intoxicating feeling of belonging to his time and to his people. Messages from liberal and radical writers poured in, and some of the more daring of them even published articles about the outrage, one entitled 'When Will This End?' appearing over the signature of none other than Maxim Gorky. Certainly the error of an illiterate detective had given Zotin more notoriety than the poems without rhyme or reason.

He volunteered for the war, knowing full well that he would be rejected on physical grounds, since he suffered from asthma. Leonid Andreyev congratulated him for his patriotic gesture and included his name in a fiery article on the contribution of the Russian artist to the war effort. Zasyadko, whose name was not mentioned since his first works had not yet been published, was meanwhile with his unit, lobbing shells at the Austrians.

The next time the two friends met was in the turmoil of 1917, when Zasyadko struggled home and Zotin repaid his debt by introducing the mild-mannered officer-on-the-run to Lunacharsky, the Soviet commissioner for education.

'Anatoli Vasilievitch, I wish to present to you Nil Lvovitch Zasyadko,' Zotin had said. 'Nil Lvovitch was forced to go to war, and became an officer owing to his superior intelligence and his knowledge of men. Even the Imperial Army was not entirely blind to elementary virtues. But at heart, Nil Lvovitch is a revolutionary, and always was one. He helped me materially when the Czarist police arrested me for writing an article attacking the autocracy, and he has always been a close friend of the toiling masses.'

Zotin was a liar, but a good-hearted one. He had even deluded himself with believing that he had actually written the article attacking the Czar, but the times were not conducive to displays of gratuitous uprightness, and so Zasyadko eagerly shook the hand of the bearded Lunacharsky, who gave him a small, insignificant post in the ministry. Here he could work quietly on his first book of any consequence, a history of the Sumerian people. It was published in 1920 and attracted the attention of scholars, but it was Zotin who was in the limelight at that period. In the same year, the Commissar Lunacharsky wrote a play entitled *Oliver Cromwell*, which conveniently forced the notorious Roundhead into the socialist mould, and Zotin followed his chief's example by bringing out a tragedy in verse about Joan of Arc called *Comrade Joan*, in which the voices the Maid of Orleans heard were the voices of the as yet unborn Marx and Engels.

Zasyadko went to the first night and thought it absurd, even blasphemous. Afterwards the two friends discussed the play through the night with that application and relentlessness which is characteristically Russian where art is concerned. Zotin was amused by Zasyadko's reservations. He spoke at length, one crude cigarette after another occupying the slot between two brown teeth which nature had unknowingly designed for his comfort.

'You, my dear Nil Lvovitch, believe that history is static, whereas I believe that it is kissed to life by a variety of Prince Charmings for every succeeding generation. I know that to your conventional, conservative mind, a Prince Charming should be dressed in blue tights and an ornamented jerkin, but you must live with the times and realize that he is now Comrade Charming, a proletarian dressed in grey, his jacket stained with honest sweat.'

Zasyadko detested this manner of argument, with its dismal imagery, and he was also weary of the discrimination between honest and dishonest sweat, which to his tidy mind was just sweat, and entirely blameless, from whatever pores it had welled. 'History is beyond your reach, Arkady Petrovitch,' he answered. 'The Sumerian people have had their day, whether we like it or not. When I wrote my history, I had before me the facts, as closely as they can be ascertained. Their story had a beginning, a middle, and an end. If scholarship should cast a new light on them, the light is only illuminating something which is there in any case. It is a discovery, but not a creation. For you to suggest that Joan of Arc heard the voice of Karl Marx is as gross a piece of nonsense as I have ever heard, and even fills the civilized spectator with a feeling of distinct malaise. The poor girl suffered death at the stake for reasons which are absolutely private. It must have been a particularly uncomfortable form of death, but if she chose it, I regard it as entirely her affair. Consequently I consider it intolerable impertinence towards someone who actually lived to suggest that she was inspired to face an ordeal by fire simply because a stuffy German professor appeared to her in a dream, and I further consider it quite unfair to poor Karl Marx to blame him for her death.'

'You are wrong,' Zotin answered, his small eyes twinkling with self-assurance and with malice. 'History is inherited like a furnished house, and we do with it what we wish. It is material which has only been left behind for us to use in influencing the present. If it will serve a political purpose for me to present Joan of Arc as a Marxist, or Martin Luther as a freethinker, I will not hesitate to do so. I am convinced that if Joan of Arc had lived now, she would have been one of us, because she was basically an intellectual in a period in which intellectuals did not exist as we know them and in which women did not carry arms as they often do now. She was an intensely modern basically Soviet woman. Her allegiance was to a King and to her voices, *faute de mieux*. History belongs to the living, Nil Lvovitch, not to the dead.'

'Nonsense,' said Zasyadko. 'You know that what success your play enjoyed tonight was not due to the characterization of Joan, which was negligible and naïve in the extreme, but to your caricatures of the priesthood, which are very much in fashion. What you perpetrated was not a distortion of history so much as a pure invention, a fantasy. Now, if we carry your thesis of the past's subservience to the whims of the present to its logical conclusion, I should ask you how you would react if, in a thousand years' time, during some great Christian revival within the framework of the Soviet state, some future Zotin writes a drama about Lenin hearing the voice of Moses, who encouraged bread rationing as the surest way of guaranteeing future milk and honey from the collective farms.'

'For goodness' sake, be careful,' muttered Zotin, and drew his chair closer to the table. 'You never know who may be listening. I regard history as a series of presents, piled on each other like plates. There is no past and no future. If the future Zotin decides that it is expedient to portray Lenin in such a way, then he will be entirely within his rights to do so.'

And so it went on, aimlessly, irreconcilably, Zasyadko always founding his arguments on a logic which he believed to be basic, a structure of thought patterns which humanity had built up by a painful process of slow advances and eliminations over the centuries; Zotin always erratically insisting that a shriek in the dark has its own value, its own beauty, and that culture is not so much an architecture as a casual kaleidoscope.

Zotin continued to write essentially noisy and blatant poetry until about 1926, when even the futurists began to lose interest in him, since he obviously lacked any quality. What he turned out was careless in the extreme and about as illuminating as a neon sign which is made to flicker in order to catch the public's attention. In 1927, the futurists themselves came under attack for formalism, and Zotin's voice was one of the loudest in condemnation of his old colleagues. He even wrote an open letter confessing his previous errors and declaring that socialism was positive and that in the future his writing would be marked by positive virtues instead of negative vices.

He applied for, and received, a grant to enable him to study tractor production with a view to initiating the new positive era of his creativity by a novel about the gratifying advances in the technique of mechanized agriculture, a subject about which he knew nothing and in which he had no great or compelling interest. He hoped, however, that his contact with a mode of living so different from his own would catapult him into some unknown stratosphere of thought and of creativity. His sojourn among the heroes of tractor production turned out to be unhappy beyond measure.

First of all, the factory was situated near the Siberian frontier, and nothing about the factory site or its environs was calculated to fire Zotin's imagination. The half-finished vehicles, like huge, wounded insects, the streams of molten steel, the piles of slag, the shafts of pale sunlight breaking into the dark vault through broken windows, the pizzicato of sparks hammering the heavy air, the sullen faces of the workmen glistening with perspiration, the ancient gramophone balefully yawning rancid waltzes in the canteen, all these were powerful, monotonous, unutterably sad impressions, and they stultified his pen with their massiveness, their gracelessness. Then technicians explained their functions to him as though he were some inspector from Moscow in disguise. They rattled off endless figures with a show of dehumanized efficiency, they sent their fingers out in great arcs on the production charts, they gave him pieces of metal to hold and explained the advantages and disadvantages of the various grades in flat voices. He took nothing in, and the only reason he stayed awake was that he knew sleep would bring unpleasant dreams with it.

Eventually he returned to Moscow, several notebooks full of facts which were relevant to tractor production but irrelevant to literature in his brief-case. In his room, he sat down before a blank sheet of paper, prepared his mind to make a start on an optimistic novel, and wept.

Over the weeks his unhappiness turned into a militant remorse. 'Do you realize,' he told Zasyadko, 'that there are people in this country of whose bitter lives we know less than nothing, you and I? How dare we go on vegetating in our furnished shelters while out there heroes, yes, heroes, labour day and night in intolerable conditions to make tractors which till the soil, and bring in the bread which we eat without a thought of them? You should go out there, among the people, instead of writing your learned volumes on ancient civilizations which nobody reads – you should go out there to refresh yourself. Go into those steel cathedrals, with their altars of lava, their candles of sparks, their priests gleaming with honest sweat.'

Yes, Zasyadko was sure there was plenty of honest sweat, but however impressed he was by the old charlatan Zotin's descriptions of the unknown world of industry, he found it absolutely impossible to read the first five chapters of the manuscript which his friend lent him.

Zotin had invented a love story between a pure socialist girl, Olga, who was supervisor of the department which fits the tracks to the tractors, and a pure socialist lad, Eygeni, who was chief of the testing team. Neither of these had any recognizable character, and the only discernible aim of their life appeared to be the raising of characterless and firmly optimistic children. They were initially thwarted in their noble plan by a riveter who was in fact a White Russian colonel bent on sowing dissatisfaction among the workers and raping Olga on the side, and by a so-called expert on industrial diesel engines who was a saboteur planted by the American Espionage Service and who studiously ruined tractor after tractor with apparent ease. There was no real light and shade in the story, since the dice were weighted heavily in favour of virtue from the very beginning, but what most thoroughly depressed Zasyadko were the long columns of statistics which Zotin had incorporated into the novel in the evident interest of authenticity. Fractions, square roots, decimal points jostled each other uncomfortably on every page, until the arithmetical symbols danced before the eyes.

All Zasyadko could say was that he never realized how adventurous the making of tractors could be. The book, entitled *The Tracks Lead to the Horizon*, appeared and was warmly welcomed by the more doctrinaire critics, who were apparently impervious to boredom, one of them even acclaiming the book as a valuable contribution to the literature of Soviet industrialization. Unfortunately there is a final arbiter of taste even in the Soviet Union, and sales were depressingly small, especially in industrial centres. The only people who really seemed to enjoy it were the tribes in Kazakhstan. This mystery was never explained, but Zotin planned to visit that republic to pay his respects for its judgment.

Meanwhile Zasyadko, who always presumed gratefully that the very nature of his occupation would take him almost out of reach of controversy, was having his own troubles. His history of the Roman Empire was bitterly attacked by another distinguished historian on the grounds that Spartacus and the revolt of the slaves were accorded quite inadequate space in the general pattern of Roman history. Zasyadko, who was never happy in controversy, declared that he respected every point of view but reserved the right to write what he felt to be the truth. Two other writers, neither of whom had made a particular study of Roman history, then proceeded to assault Zasyadko for 'being more interested in his own opinions than in history'.

During this unpleasant period, Zasyadko tended to withdraw from circulation. For a time he was tempted to write about the French Revolution, an upheaval which had interested him deeply ever since his youth, but then he thought better of it, since he had no desire to glorify an unscrupulous villain like Marat, after whom the Russians had named a battleship. Instead he turned his attentions to Charlemagne, about whom there had been very few proletarian theories. Living quietly in a little *dacha* with his devoted wife, he worked painstakingly and all but lost sight of Zotin.

Time passed, and Zotin, frustrated by his inability to be realistic, optimistic, and commercial at the same time, took refuge where so many Soviet writers have sought a haven, in translation. Unfortunately his knowledge of foreign languages was very incomplete, and it was consequently particularly rash of him to make an attempt at the works of Rabindranath Tagore. After struggling for eight months with the aid of three dictionaries and an Indian student, he published a short poem in a magazine, but it was brutally attacked on the grounds of 'decadent mysticism'. Russia was not yet interested in Indian culture, since the British were still in possession, and Zotin gave up the unequal struggle. Briefly he explored the other escape road of Soviet literature and wrote a book for children, *The Kulak and the Big Red Bear*, but since he knew nothing of children and in fact detested them, the children could hardly help sensing this and invariably burst into fitful tears when the garish, angular morality was read to them at bedtime. After a time the volume was preserved only as a punishment, or at least as a deterrent, in a few homes.

Criticism and neglect produced quite the opposite effect on Zotin than on Zasyadko. Far from retiring, he attended every writers' meeting wherever it was held and was more evident in person than in print. His hair had turned white, his face was a mass of contradictory wrinkles which gave him an ambiguous expression, somewhere between grief and savage joy, his mouth had but one tooth left in it, like a rusty buoy in a dark estuary. His fingers, his beard, and his lips were stained with nicotine, and the glasses he now wore did not seem to help him see any better, since his eyes were always screwed up as though he were in pain. Like an old dog, he sniffed the wind, recognized the scents, but refrained from barking.

Just after the outbreak of the so-called Patriotic War, Zasyadko published the book which was to bring him fame, a history of the Teutonic knights. He had finished it in 1940, but he could hardly let it appear at a time when Russia and Germany were allies and the conflicting creeds of communism and fascism were linked in an awkward and callous liaison. Zasyadko showed surprising practicality in biding his time, for no sooner had Hitler embarked on his invasion of Russia than this thick volume about German territorial ambition and brutality in the thirteenth century became a best seller, full of a gratuitous symbolism which the times themselves supplied. He became an academician, was heaped with honours, and had an agreeable chat with Stalin.

Once again it was his turn to take Zotin under his wing, and, using his now considerable influence, he procured his old friend some commissions to write patriotic poems for the newspapers. Zotin managed this quite well, since critical standards are subservient to emotion in times of peril. After the war, Zotin attempted to write a book about the war against the Germans and the Finns, but although the facts in it were accurate, he had never served in the Army, nor had he ever been north of Leningrad, and a certain woodenness inevitably resulted. The rapid restoration of normal relations with Finland did not help him either, and for these many reasons *On to the Baltic, Comrades* was a failure.

It was a bitter man who vociferously applauded the degrading stipulations of Comrade Zhdanov at the 1946 Congress, when that acrid and talentless theorist demanded a literature saturated with enthusiasm and heroism. Zotin was now sixty-seven years old, and he determined to go out in search of those elusive qualities if it was the last thing he ever did.

'What Zhdanov says is quite true,' he explained to Zasyadko, while sipping a glass of kvass on the latter's veranda, 'and he explains it well. There can be no more conflict in our Soviet literature, since conflict suggests good and evil, and evil is now so rare that there is no point in showing it. It is untypical, you understand. The only conflict which can possibly exist is a conflict between good and better. Consequently, since the aim of our new literature is enthusiasm and heroism, it stands to reason that the only conflict can be between enthusiasm and ecstasy, mere bravery and heroism. It certainly opens up entirely new panoramas to us.'

Zasyadko laughed. 'For an intelligent man,' he said, 'you are a remarkable ass.'

Zotin looked offended. 'I did not say that. It was Comrade Zhdanov.'

'That surprises me less,' said Zasyadko.

Zotin smiled. 'You were clever to bring out your book on the Teutonic knights when you did,' he said.

'How sad that we should have to think in terms of expediency in such matters.' Zasyadko sighed. 'I could not have published it before, and who knows, soon it may be out of date once again. It depends not on historical truth, but on which way our friends the Germans jump.'

Zotin smiled childishly. 'Nil Lvovitch,' he said, 'help me to find a subject.'

'One which is both enthusiastic and heroic?'

'Yes.'

Zasyadko's wife had died in 1943, and since her death the two ageing men had seen a great deal of each other. They reminded each other of so much that was now lost irretrievably. Zasyadko laughed. In spite of the fact that he found much in Zotin to despise, he could not help liking him.

'How about an autobiography?' he asked.

'Now you are laughing at me.'

'Yes.'

'I am a great coward, both morally and physically – yes, and even artistically – but that will not prevent me from writing a most enthusiastic, most heroic book, which will surprise you.'

'I wait with bated breath.'

Zotin made six different beginnings, but abandoned them all because he felt they were deficient in those properties which were officially demanded of them. He found it extremely difficult to write without conflict and began to hanker after that lost galaxy of saboteurs, spies, and counter-revolutionaries which had been so useful to Soviet writers before.

'What on earth would Pushkin have done?' Zotin asked Zasyadko.

The Germans had fulfilled the necessary function during the war, but now there was nothing but unrelieved virtue to play with, roll into a ball, and fire enthusiastically and heroically at the critics.

'I'll tell you exactly,' came the reply. 'Pushkin would have translated all of Shakespeare, all of Byron, all of Keats, all of Shelley, and if he ever ran out of material, he would have taken his own life after shooting Zhdanov.'

'You can afford to talk like that, you're an academician,' Zotin said ruefully.

'Not because I am an academician, but because I am alone with you.'

The desperate Zotin even paid a visit to Kazakhstan but found nobody who had read his book there. It fired neither his enthusiasm nor his sense of the heroic.

In 1953, when Zotin was seventy-four and Zasyadko seventy-six, Stalin died. Suddenly everyone could breathe again, but as they were not used to it, relief took time to become apparent. The next year, the journalist Ehrenburg published his book, *The Thaw*, and it looked as though a new era in Soviet letters was beginning, more especially since the vituperative Ehrenburg is really a cautious man, a professional survivor disguised as a firebrand, a man whose brilliant intelligence, pressed into devious and diplomatic channels, wears only the outer mask of frankness and whose steady eye hides a nervously opportunistic mind.

Zasyadko saw less of Zotin during this time of emancipation, and it was clear to him that the old rascal was engaged in some creative activity or other. Then the arteries of freedom hardened once again, and the creative blood congealed. Zotin seemed to be a broken man. He talked very little, he was hard up, he was sullenly impatient for death. Nothing that Zasyadko could say or do would cheer him up.

Zasyadko worked quietly on his book about the Assyrians, and once again Zotin drifted away from him until one memorable day when an old, old man suddenly arrived at the *dacha*, haggard, wizened, yet reinvested with all the mischief of his youth. Zasyadko hardly recognized him.

'Nil Lvovitch, some most surprising news!'

'Good God, Arkady Petrovitch, where do you spring from? I thought you were dead.'

'I have been pretending to be dead.'

'Judging from your appearance, you have pretended very convincingly.'

'Yes. I lost my tooth.'

Over a cup of tea, Zotin explained that there was a rumour that Pasternak had written a book, entitled *Doctor Zhivago*.

'That's nothing new,' Zasyadko answered. 'Boris Leonidovitch has been working on it for years.'

'It has been refused.'

'That's nothing new either.'

'No, but it has been accepted by an Italian publisher, and sold to France, England, and America! America!'

'Why should that excite you?' asked Zasyadko. 'It won't do Boris Leonidovitch any good. On the contrary.'

'Nil Lvovitch, I am seventy-nine years of age,' pleaded Zotin. 'I don't care any more for my safety, and as for my reputation, you know as well as I do that I have none to lose. All my life I have vacillated. I was a false futurist, a false realist, a bad poet, a hopeless translator, an impossible writer for children, but I am not stupid, Nil Lvovitch. I am not stupid.'

There were tears forming in Zasyadko's eyes as he echoed, 'No, you're not stupid.'

'I have seen a great many things in my time. I have a good memory, and I love writing. It is my only passion. I never even married, because I formed a monastic attachment to my desk. Well, let me tell you something. You didn't see much of me after Stalin died. I wrote the only important work I had it in me to write: my confessions, the confessions of a time-server, of a coward, of a crank. I put it all down, all. I spared myself no humiliation in the interest of truth. I exposed myself, and with it I exposed the futurists, the formalists, the petty theorists, Zhdanov, Stalin, the whole odious conspiracy which has made a mockery of Russian letters and the Russian language, that which should be finest, that which Pushkin, Lermontov, Nekrasov, Dostoevsky, Turgenev, Tolstoy used to spin their magic webs of sound and meaning. Alas, I am old. I could not write fast enough. Before I had finished, the freedom was gone again, and the outlets were sealed. Now, if I could have published in Italy . . .'

There was a pause, and then both old men began crying bitterly, like children.

Before long, the news of Pasternak's success abroad began to filter through to Soviet writers, and this was followed by the award of the Nobel Prize, gracefully accepted. The consternation in Moscow was followed by an equally graceful, but far sadder refusal of the honour by the author, and there was a large meeting at which a young functionary, by name Semichastny, compared Pasternak to a pig. Khrushchev, who was present, was seen to clap loudly at this scintillating display of subtlety, along with everyone else. It was a striking demonstration of party solidarity in the face of the grim menace of quality and international approval.

Afterwards, Zotin went to visit Zasyadko and said, 'Glory to Boris Leonidovitch. He has really demonstrated that the pen is mightier than the sword. Zhukov went without a murmur, Molotov disappeared overnight, God only knows what has happened to poor Bulganin, Beria vanished like a raindrop in the sunlight, but here's a mere author, and what a rumpus he has created with nothing but his vision, a tiny pen five inches long, and a few sheets of paper. I tell you, Nil Lvovitch, it is a victory of the individual over the amorphous crowd.'

'I agree,' said Zasyadko. 'For a country which has condemned the cult of personality, we are curiously paradoxical. We are practically the only nation which names ships, streets, automobile factories, and even whole towns after living people. If that isn't a cult of personality, then for god's sake what is?'

'That's why they have to keep changing the names of our streets, ships, and cities so often,' Zotin added. 'But to return to the meeting. It was really quite degrading. Considering that Boris Leonidovitch's book has never been published here, an awful lot of people seem to have read it. Even our revered secretary applauded loudly when that young fellow Semichastny called Boris Leonidovitch a pig, and I somehow don't believe that he would have had time to read the manuscript, since he is so busy writing letters to Eisenhower himself.'

'The standards of Russian criticism have never been high.'

'Hang the critics,' said Zotin excitedly. 'Think of Pasternak's glory – to be called a pig and to have that opinion endorsed by a gathering of our greatest, most heroic, most enthusiastic leaders, who, on top of everything, have never read the book in question. My dear Nil Lvovitch, that even transcends glory, that is martyrdom.'

'And you're jealous?'

'Yes, I am,' admitted Zotin.

A few days later, Zotin presented himself at the Italian Embassy. To the surprised cultural attaché he revealed his whole extravagant story. The attaché, being both cultural and Italian, was extremely courteous and promised to dispatch the huge and dishevelled manuscript to the publisher who had so nobly set Pasternak on his road to Calvary. Zotin left in high spirits, and he seemed to become younger by the day. In case anyone had seen him visit the Italian Embassy, he told everyone that he was embarking on a vast trilogy about the Risorgimento and that he had gone for some technical books.

There was no trouble of any sort, and the days passed

in eager anticipation of news. Then one morning it was no longer the impish Zotin who appeared at the gate of Zasyadko's *dacha,* but a broken man, clutching a huge manuscript which seemed far too heavy for him to carry.

'What's the matter?' Zasyadko cried.

'Read this. You're good at languages,' Zotin answered in a small, dull voice.

Zasyadko took the letter which was attached to the manuscript, and read it. It was in French.

'It doesn't really matter what it says,' Zotin murmured as Zasyadko was reading. 'The fact is they sent the manuscript back, and that's enough.'

'It says that it isn't the kind of book they're looking for,' Zasyadko said. 'They find it interesting, but too diffuse and too violent in parts to be effective.'

The colour came back to Zotin's face. 'Damn them, damn them, damn those Westerners with their haughty ways. Who the hell do they think they are?'

'It is unfortunate,' said Zasyadko, for want of something better.

'Unfortunate,' howled Zotin. 'I am a Russian writer, d'you hear me? A Russian writer, worth ten Gabriele d'Annunzios. How dare they treat me like some local upstart! How dare they explain their rejection at all!'

'You are making the classical mistake of all of us Russians,' said Zasyadko firmly, even angrily. 'Either we fawn towards the West or we insult it. We can never treat it as an equal. Either we all talk bad French to each other, as in the old days, or we call French an inferior language. Either we imitate their technology, or we consider it beneath contempt. We accept the Nobel Prize for our scientists and refuse it for our authors. When will this ridiculous complex end? In the past we attacked Tchaikovsky because he was not Russian enough and scoffed at Glinka because he was too Russian. We have not changed a bit. To be Russian is no better and no worse than to be anything else – it is just different. Why can't we accept it?'

Zotin was furious. 'To be Russian is to be better than anything else,' he cried.

'Yesterday it was to be worse than anything else, according to you. You couldn't wait until you were recognized abroad.'

'You are a Westerner and a traitor!' Zotin sobbed.

'No, Arkady Petrovitch, the trouble is in yourself, you good, foolish man. There is one thing you never learned, and that is to take your time. To be in a hurry is to kill your talent. Dear friend, to reach the sun it is not enough to jump into the air.'

Zotin looked at Zasyadko reproachfully, and left.

Zasyadko became aware of a silence, and his daydream ended. Looking round, he noticed that the eyes of everyone in the room were on him. Comrade Grigalka was still on the podium, and it was clear that the diatribe against Pasternak had just ended. Everyone, including Grigalka, was staring at him because he must have been the only one who had not joined in the storm of applause which traditionally greets a speech of high moral tenor.

'Well,' he thought, 'I'm eighty-one, after all. They'll have to excuse me on account of my age.'

The pause continued with unabated intensity, and Grigalka's glasses glittered once again. Zasyadko was even less for controversy in his old age than he had been when he was younger. He had only come to this accursed meeting in order to make sure that poor Arkady Petrovitch didn't make a fool of himself. He was too old and too tired to care whether Boris Leonidovitch was a pig, or a hyena, or not. In any case, he preferred animals to human beings on the whole. He made one last concession by bringing his two hands together like a pistol shot, once. Then he stared at Zotin from under his white eyebrows, but Zotin looked away.

# ADD A DASH OF PITY

'You really are a great procrastinator,' said Philip Hedges.

John Otford fidgeted in his swivel chair and smiled non-committally. It was a beautiful late autumn day. The sun caught the shivering golden leaves, while the slight breeze made their shadows caress the rows of ancient books which lined the walls of his study. Near the window, particles of dust floated idly in various directions.

'I'm lazy, I admit it,' said Otford briefly, 'but then the nature of my work is distinctly devitalizing, and anyway, I feel like golf.'

'I do too,' Hedges sighed, 'but I daren't give in to temptation. We go to press in ten days.'

'Oh, you and your encyclopedia, why can't you just reprint what I wrote five years ago? I sweated blood to get my stuff ready then.'

'If you read my letter, which I doubt,' said Hedges, with a touch of friendly acidity, 'you may remember that we had no wish to alter your admirable and scholarly piece on Oliver Cromwell's battles or on Napoleon in Egypt, but since the Italian campaign in the recent war has been mentioned so frequently in the memoirs of generals, some new facts have come to light which may bear consideration.'

'Memoirs of generals,' snorted Otford. 'Most of them are damn bad writers, or at least show the same lack of discrimination in selecting their ghost writers as they do in selecting their staff officers.'

'I don't know how you can say that,' said Hedges. 'The copies of the books I sent you years ago for your perusal are still here, on your table, under a handsome coating of dust. Patton's book, Mark Clark's, Omar Bradley's, Eisenhower's, Manstein's! I see Monty's is on top. Is there any symbolism in this?'

'It was the last to arrive.' Otford became a little impatient. 'Philip,' he said, 'you're a dear fellow, but I wish you'd leave me alone. The piece I wrote about the Italian campaign was extremely painstaking, well documented, and, I flatter myself, written in pure and sober style. In spite of your aspersions, I did skim through these books when they first arrived, and, quite frankly, they do not alter a single known fact. Now, to cap it all, you bring me a five-hundred-page epic, hot from the press, the dull adventures of Sir Crowdson Gribbell, a thoroughly undistinguished officer, whose only claim to fame is to have engineered the passage of the Rizzio River against vastly inferior enemy forces.'

'John, you're impossible.' Hedges laughed.

Otford picked up General Gribbell's book and glanced at the cover with distaste. 'Look at this ludicrous cover, Philip, a face so undistinguished it is impossible to forget, framed against a montage of burning tanks and retreating men, probably his own. *Those Were My Orders,* he calls it. A marvellous, equivocal phrase. No doubt when events went in his favour, he could reflect that the action was successful because those were his orders, and they were obeyed, whereas when things went against him, he could shrug his shoulders and say, "Those were my orders," and blame those who guided his destinies and against whose follies he had no power. It's a marvellous title, when you consider it. So typical of the Army. It means nothing, and everything. It's grandiloquent, and yet it doesn't commit the author. Full marks to Gribbell on his title, anyway. It's like a shout of triumph in a soundproof room.'

'You're remarkably cynical for a military historian.'

'It is impossible to be a military historian without being

cynical, my dear fellow. If I had the time and wasn't by nature very indolent, I could write a tome as weighty as ten encyclopedias solely on the mistakes of generals. Napoleon, Blücher, Marlborough, Ney, they all made the most flagrant and unforgivable errors of judgment.'

'Could you have done better?'

Otford smiled sweetly. 'Of course not, that's why I'm a military historian, not a soldier.'

Hedges tried again. He became very serious.

'What about it, John?'

'Why don't you get someone else?'

'Because when you put your mind to it, you're a thoroughly entertaining writer, quite apart from being a penetrating scholar.'

'Stop flattering me.'

'And you're not going to tell me you haven't plenty of time to do it. Every time I come here, I find you sitting in your office, staring out of your window, with an expression on your face which suggests that you blame mankind for not being in the South of France.'

John grinned. He recognized the portrait of himself. 'It's no joke, being the keeper of arms and armour in a great museum,' he said. 'All you've got to do is to keep the relics clean. The Greeks, Egyptians, Romans, and the rest of them did all the work for me. There's nothing to create. Previous generations of curators compiled the stuff, and now, with the present financial stringencies, I have no allocation to buy anything new. The great difficulty in my job is keeping awake.'

'Then you admit you have the time to do other work.'

'I admit I have the time,' said Otford, 'but I don't have the inclination.'

Just then Mr Pole knocked and entered. He was an old man, charged with preventing warlike children from stealing the scimitars and halberds from the museum. He wore a dark blue uniform, with a pair of golden crowns on his collar.

'That woman's here again, sir,' he said.

Otford blanched. 'Send her away.'

'She won't go. Both Mr Elvis and Sergeant Oakie have tried to get her to go, but she's most persistent, to put it mildly.'

'Tell her I've gone.'

'She saw your car, sir.'

'How did she know it was mine?'

'I don't know, sir, but she said it was yours, and I couldn't very well deny it. She knew the number. KXR 759.'

Hedges laughed. 'A woman?' he said. 'Maybe I can blackmail you into revising that article. Does Jean know?'

'It's no joking matter,' Otford muttered. 'For the last two days she's been making my life a misery, calling every quarter of an hour, either by phone or in person.'

'Who is she?'

'Blowed if I know. A Mrs Allen or Alban or something.'

'Mrs Alban,' said Mr Pole. 'A Mrs Alaric Alban.'

'I'll leave by the back way, Pole,' Otford said, 'and perhaps you could ask Sergeant Oakie to bring the car round into Treadington Mews.'

'What do I do in the meanwhile, sir?' asked Pole. 'The poor lady seems very upset. She's sitting down in the Etruscan room. I had to get her a glass of water.'

'Use your initiative, Pole,' Otford answered vaguely.

Hedges was puzzled. 'But why are you so scared of her, John?'

'She's thoroughly hysterical on the phone, incoherent even.'

Hedges smiled. 'I thought that sort of thing only

happened to film stars and crooners. What did she say, or is that secret?'

'It's very secret. She kept it to herself. I didn't understand a word, except that it's something to do with her husband.'

'Her husband?'

'That's funny,' said Pole suddenly, staring at the copy of Sir Crowdson Gribbell's autobiography, which Otford had replaced on his desk. 'Every time she's been here, she's been clutching a copy of that book.'

'Are you sure?' Otford asked.

'Positive.'

'That doesn't seem very suitable reading for a hysterical woman,' said Hedges. 'How old is she?'

'In her fifties, I'd say, sir.'

'She may be one of Gribbell's discarded mistresses from Old Delhi,' muttered Otford, intrigued in spite of himself.

'What was her name again?' asked Hedges.

'Alban. Mrs Alaric Alban,' said Pole.

In silence, Hedges opened the book and thumbed through the index. Suddenly his eyebrows rose in surprise.

'Well?'

'Alban, Brigadier Alaric, later colonel, page 347. Brigadier, later colonel. That's curious.'

Hedges found page 347 and cleared his throat.

'It was 29th November,' he read, 'when my division had already been holding the line of the River Rizzio for rather more than a month, that one of those rare incidents occurred which cast their pall over a soldier's career, and force him to take decisions which, however disagreeable they may be, are necessary to the success of a campaign—'

'Pompous ass,' interrupted Otford. 'I can just hear him dictating that.'

'On the evening of the 28th, I returned by light airplane from protracted discussions with General Mark Clark, who had asked me whether, in my opinion, it would be possible for me to launch a full-scale attack in concert with the Polish Division on my right flank on a very narrow front, the idea being to ford the Rizzio and seize the road junction of San Melcchore di Stetto, thereby splitting the enemy line at a vital point. The Polish general was willing, but I remonstrated, believing that our troops were in no condition to do more than hold the line until we had properly built up our supplies to ensure success. Intelligence had ascertained that there were elements of two enemy divisions on the north bank, the 381st and the crack Grosser Kurfürst Grenadiers, and I was certainly opposed to any unnecessary waste of life which a rash and unprepared attack against a formidable opponent would most surely entail. The American general, while remaining courteous, was most insistent in trying to engage my support for his plan, and I was not helped by the rash and even boastful attitude of the Polish commander, who indulged in the most unnecessary braggadocio. I told General Clark I would give him my answer within twenty-four hours, and left for my headquarters in the hamlet of Valendazzo. The atmosphere at my departure was somewhat unpleasant, but restrained. Upon arrival at Valendazzo, I immediately asked my brigade commanders to dinner. Freddy Archer-Brown, my aide-de-camp, and Tom Hawley, my intelligence officer, were also present. Brigadier Foulis supported my plan entirely, the only opposition coming from Brigadier Alban, an officer with a fine record of personal courage but of a somewhat unbalanced and turbulent disposition. Brigadier Alban became very aggressive in the course of dinner, and told me I didn't know what I was doing. He left headquarters in high dudgeon, and the next morning, acting entirely on his own initiative, he launched a local attack without the benefit of artillery support, and although two companies

managed to get a precarious foothold on the further bank
of the river, the casualties were enormous and I was forced
to bring them back. Brigadier Alban was court-martialled
and retired with the rank of colonel. This was a generous
verdict, and only made possible by his record of high
personal courage.'

There was a pause. Otford frowned.

'D'you feel like seeing her now, Sherlock?' asked
Hedges.

'Gribbell was probably right,' said Otford.

'How unlike you.'

'Pole, bring the lady in.'

Pole left the room briefly, and then returned.

'She's gone,' he said.


There was no trace of an Alaric Alban in the phone book,
and so that evening, instead of going straight home, Otford
went to a club in St James's Street. He tried to pretend
to himself that he was only going there for a drink, but in
truth his sense of adventure had been stirred. The club
was one to which he had been elected some time ago but
which he had never frequented, because it reminded him
too acutely of his public school. The members, mostly
superannuated military with a smattering of the prematurely old, had never liberated themselves from the
hierarchical aspects of their scholastic lives. They sat
around in deep chairs with hostile expressions on their
faces, trying to assess their exact positions in the scheme
of things from the relative servility or arrogance of other
faces.

Otford entered, left his hat in the cloakroom, and
strolled through the ample rooms as though looking for
someone. There was a churchlike murmur of soft conversation. The carpet absorbed his feet as he walked. He
veered away from the bar, since no less than three notori-

ous bores were seated there, waiting for victims like street-walkers in a dive. Eventually he spotted Leopard Bately seated alone in the reading-room, glancing at a magazine devoted to horse racing. Not a bad chap, the Leopard, a major-general on the active list. He was a man with a febrile military imagination and a private fortune to back up the most outrageous ideas and make of his career a hobby. His rather grand nickname had not sprung from any exceptional deeds of valour, but rather from the fact that he had been dogged by a skin disease from youth.

'Good evening, sir.'

The Leopard looked up and smiled. 'Otford, we don't have the pleasure of seeing you here very often.'

'May I join you?'

'By all means. I'm only killing time, and I find I'm damn bad at it.'

Over a Scotch and soda, Otford asked him if he'd ever known a Brigadier Alban.

The Leopard frowned. 'Alaric Alban? Yes. Unfortunate affair that. Had it coming to him though. Couldn't have ended any other way.'

'Was he a bad soldier?'

'Oh no, too good by half. And a half's too large a margin to be good by, if you understand me. What happened to him nearly happened to me on more than one occasion. And then – I don't really know whether he drank excessively, didn't know him well enough for that, but he always seemed to be drunk. He had a kind of slurred speech and a bleary eye and the very devil of a temper. I think he was probably allergic to stupidity, and if you're allergic to stupidity in the Army you take a drink, and eventually, you blow your top at the wrong moment and find yourself a bitter, disagreeable civilian.'

'D'you think that'll happen to you?'

'Lord no, I'm not allergic to stupidity. I'm amused by it. I'll probably end up a field-marshal.'

After a slight pause, Otford asked the Leopard, 'Have you read Gribbell's book, by any chance?'

'Gribbell's book, did you say? Didn't know the fellow could write.'

'It was probably written for him.'

'No, I've got better things to do than to embark on a voyage of discovery into a thoroughly mediocre mind.'

The copy of *The Times* opposite them lowered, and they found themselves fixed by a pair of eyes remarkable for their lack of expression.

'We were just discussing your book, sir,' Otford stammered.

'My book? It's only been out two days.'

'I've read most of it already,' said Otford.

'It's a fascinating story, isn't it?' answered Gribbell as a statement of fact.

'I haven't read it,' said the Leopard with some irritation.

'What's that?'

'I haven't read it.'

'I think you'll like it, Bately, makes fine reading.'

Otford bit his lip, and took the plunge. 'The description of the fording of the Rizzio threw an entirely new light on the Italian campaign,' he said.

Gribbell's face became almost kind, even grateful. He put his newspaper down. 'Are you a soldier, sir?' he asked.

'I'm a historian.'

'Military?'

'Yes. My name's John Otford.'

Gribbell did not react to this. He seemed to hear only what he wished to hear, and when John revealed his identity, the general was already thinking of his own next phrase. 'You know,' he said, 'some of you fellows have been confoundedly unfair to some of us, the poor saps who actually did the fighting.'

'Isn't it true to say that some of you fighting fellows have been confoundedly unfair to each other? Having read Ike and Blood-and-Guts and Monty and Omar Bradley, I think it's a wonder we won at all.'

Gribbell didn't hear this. 'Nobody has ever realized,' he went on, 'that if I hadn't crossed the Rizzio when I did, on Christmas Day, we might all still be in Italy to this day.' He smiled wanly, and seemed to be waiting for congratulations.

'What if you had attacked when Mark Clark wanted you to attack?'

Gribbell treated this question as an impertinence. 'My dear young sir,' he said with surprising venom, 'if I had done as I was told, I'd have lost two thousand men for no reason.'

'And what if you had supported Brigadier Alban's attack?'

Gribbell rose to his feet as though his face had been slapped. 'I didn't come here to be insulted,' he said stiffly. 'May I ask if you are a guest at this club, or a member?'

'A member,' John replied steadily.

'I am extremely sorry to hear it.'

Gribbell stalked off.

'Full marks,' murmured the Leopard.

And suddenly Gribbell was back. 'There are certain things a man cannot put into a book because of the libel laws,' he said, more reasonably. 'There's one aspect of Alban's attack which I couldn't mention. The man was drunk. He led the attack in pyjamas.'

As Otford drove home, his mind was working under great pressure. He had to make a conscious effort to obey the red and green lights. Why had General Gribbell taken such an exaggerated degree of offence at the mention of

Alban's name? And why had he made such an impressive, if conventional, exit, only to ruin it by returning with a comparatively rational explanation of Alban's behaviour? What strange importance he had given the whole event by his extreme of anger and his gratuitous explanation for it!

Otford parked his car and was about to switch off the lights, when he fancied he saw a woman standing flush with the hedge about thirty yards away. After a momentary hesitation, he did switch off the lights, got out, and locked the car. Then he waited. He thought he heard the noise of a heel shifting on gravel, and then all was silent.

'Mrs Alban,' he called.

Silence.

He opened the door of the car again, turned the ignition key, and slowly edged forward in the pitch darkness. Suddenly he switched on the headlamps, and there was a miserable, white-faced woman caught in the beam. She was grasping a copy of *Those Were My Orders*. Otford braked, opened the door, and said, 'Mrs Alban, would you care for a drink?' in as casual a voice as he could muster.

'Why do you keep running away from me?' she blurted.

'I didn't realize who you were.'

'You're laughing at me!'

'Why should I laugh at you?' Otford was a little taken aback. For a moment, neither knew what to say.

'Do come in, where we can talk in peace and quiet.'

Jean Otford was furious because her husband had failed to phone that he would be late for dinner, and, when he finally appeared, he was not alone but with a dishevelled lady who looked like a vagrant.

They ate dinner in silence, a barrier of fury separating husband and wife, and Mrs Alban adding fuel to the mute discord by remarking that the food was excellent, that she had had no intention of staying to dinner but that

Otford had insisted, and that she had missed her last connection to Sunningdale, and what could she do?

After coffee, Jean stamped out of the room, not having said a word, and Otford turned to Mrs Alban. 'Tell me,' he said, 'why have you repeatedly telephoned me and badgered me for the last two days?'

'I'm afraid your wife is not very pleased with me,' Mrs Alban observed, meekly.

'It's me she's not very pleased with, even if you happened to be the cause. I wish you'd answer my question.'

'Did you ever meet my husband?' she asked, with evident difficulty. She was a highly nervous woman and not very appealing.

'No.'

'Well, I don't suppose you've read this book.'

'I have, yes.'

'Oh.'

She paused. Otford felt he knew what was coming, but she was having to consider how to present her case, and it took time. She was pitiful, almost a harridan, her eyes bloodshot, her white hair dishevelled.

'You read about Brigadier Alban, then.'

'Yes.'

'Do you believe it?'

'I have no reason not to.'

Mrs Alban began to cry, but curiously enough she evoked very little sympathy, so much did tears seem to be a normal feature of her face. 'It's unfair,' she cried, 'utterly unfair.'

'Were you there?' asked Otford, a little surprised at his own toughness. Curiously enough this pathetic woman was irritating him.

'Of course I wasn't there, but I know Ric, I know my husband.'

She was so defiant that Otford felt slightly guilty, but

just looked down and waited. After all, this woman had caused a row between him and his wife, she had eaten his food, why should he help her to end her long, embarrassing pauses?

'I know my husband, and I know Crowdy Gribbell.'

'Oh?' Otford looked up sharply. 'Where did you know him?'

'India, Mesopotamia, I know both him and Flora. I was at school with Flora. We were cousins, vaguely.'

'Flora? Mrs Gribbell?'

'Lady Gribbell,' Mrs Alban corrected. Even enemies must be given their due in England. 'A selfish, opinionated, greedy woman if ever there was one.'

Yes, even enemies must be given their due. Mrs Alban passed a hand across her face as though trying to make a fresh start. 'Crowdy was two years older than Ric, but Ric overtook him very quickly. My husband won a D.S.O. and bar in 1917, when he was only eighteen years of age. He fought in Estonia against the Bolsheviks and then joined Ironside in Archangel. At the age of twenty-four, he was a captain in India, while Crowdy was only a stick-in-the-mud lieutenant with the 1st Battalion of his regiment in the North of England. They served together in the Madras region in the early thirties. Ric was the youngest major but one in the Army, while Crowdy Gribbell was an acting captain, in charge of a company of foot-sloggers. At the outbreak of war, my husband was forty-one. He was a lieutenant-colonel in charge of a regiment of armoured cars. Crowdy was forty-three then. He was still a captain, and talking of retirement. Ric was captured at Dunkirk, but escaped. It was one of the most spectacular escapes of the war, but he never wrote about it, nor would he even speak about it. In the winter of 1940, he was back in England, full of ideas about how to hit the

Huns hard, where it would hurt them most. In 1941, he led a raid of eight volunteers on to the Channel Islands and captured a vital piece of German equipment. He was congratulated and reprimanded in the same breath.'

'Why?' Otford asked.

'He didn't tell anyone he was going. Later that year they gave him an armoured brigade in Ethiopia, and he pushed far ahead of the main Army, capturing six Italian generals and all their men. In 1942, there was talk of his getting a division, but nothing came of it. He lost his temper with all the wrong people, Jumbo Wilson, the Secretary for War. He was given a desk job in the War Office until he took over the 241st Brigade, but by then Crowdy Gribbell had crept up in his unspectacular way, and poor Ric found himself under the orders of the very man he least wanted to have anything to do with.'

'They hated each other?'

'I don't think Ric really hated Crowdy. They had had some pretty bitter rows in the past, but Ric isn't a vindictive man. He hated what Crowdy stands for rather than Crowdy himself; the dull, the unadventurous, the servile. "Why on earth did a man like that ever join the Army?" he used to say.'

'In order to become a general was the answer,' said Otford, who found this kind of military wife jarring. 'But tell me, please, in your desire to clear your husband, why did you come to me?'

'I looked you up in the back of the encyclopedia at the public library. You wrote about the campaign in Italy. You see, Ric will never write a book. If he did, no one would ever publish it. But you do write the one authoritative commentary which everyone can read. It is part of the record.'

Just then Jean burst in. She was in a nightdress and bathrobe.

'Are you coming to bed?' she asked.

For a moment, Otford felt tempted to flare up. Instead he answered very casually, 'In a moment, my dear. I'm just going to drive Mrs Alban to Sunningdale.'

To Jean the idea of a journey to Sunningdale at that hour of the night was so preposterous it was almost comic. She just slammed the door.

The journey took much longer than Otford had imagined, and all the while Mrs Alban droned on, venting all the sour emotions of a regimental Lady Macbeth. She referred endlessly to the injustice which had befallen her husband, but she never produced a shred of evidence to prove that Gribbell hadn't been justified in his actions.

When they eventually reached the low shack in which Mrs Alban said she lived, the front door was open and a tall, gaunt figure stood silhouetted against the light of the hallway.

'Oh, dear,' muttered Mrs Alban, genuinely alarmed.

'Where the hell have you been?' shouted the colonel.

'Mr Otford was kind enough to bring me back,' she said nervously.

'Otford? Are you the stuffed shirt who wrote all that pompous drivel about the Italian show in the encyclopedia?'

'How did you know?' asked his wife, surprised.

'Yes,' said Otford.

'And I suppose,' the colonel went on, 'that my wife has been badgering you with a lot of tearful tales about me.'

Otford glanced at Mrs Alban and felt for her, perhaps for the first time. She looked so utterly desperate, so lost, so betrayed. 'It is I, Colonel Alban, who have been badgering her.'

'I don't believe it.'

Otford got out of the car. He felt it was more dignified.

The colonel, he noticed, was in pyjamas. There was a smell of whisky in the wind.

'You can believe what you damn well like,' snapped Otford, surprising even himself by his courage. 'The fact is that I am interested in the crossing of the Rizzio, and as a historian I want to find out what I can from whatever source possible.'

'I don't know why you've got out of your car,' the colonel retorted. 'If you think I'm going to ask you in you're very much mistaken, and if you cherish an illusion that I'm going to thank you for bringing my wife back safely, you're even more mistaken. I couldn't possibly care less where she's been, what she does, or whether I ever see her again. The same, sir, goes for you.' He suddenly aimed a fairly powerful blow at his wife, which missed her, although whether it missed her by intention or miscalculation was not clear. With a little moan, she vanished into the shack. One or two windows opened in neighbouring houses, and sleepy people shouted for a bit of quiet.

'And now,' said the colonel, 'clear out, hop it, vamoose.'

'I'm beginning to believe what Sir Crowdson Gribbell told me,' Otford called after the vanishing figure. 'You got the sack because you were drunk!'

The colonel turned and came back slowly. In a quiet voice, he said, 'Quite correct. I was drunk as a lord. Not only was I drunk, but I was wearing pyjamas on that particular occasion, white ones with a thin blue stripe. I led an attack in disobedience to orders and was broken by a court martial, a fate which I richly deserved. General Sir Crowdson Gribbell knew what he was doing, and I did not. The result of my precipitate action cost us four hundred and twenty-four men killed and nearly eight hundred wounded. Satisfied?'

Slowly and a little unsteadily, he walked back to his front door.

Otford, chastened, said, 'I hope, sir, that you won't take my foolishness out on your wife.'

'That,' replied the colonel, 'like the battle of the River Rizzio, is my business.' And he closed the door.

Otford arrived home at four in the morning, tired, irritated, and baffled. He tiptoed into his bedroom and undressed as silently as possible. As he grew accustomed to the dark, he became conscious of the fact that his wife was looking at him with large, hurt eyes. He was too upset to attempt any explanation at that late hour, so he pretended not to see her and lay still in the dark, feigning sleep.

The next morning there was a coldness at breakfast, and even then Otford did not have the stomach to end it. He could somehow think clearer in the strained silence. He left for the office without saying good-bye.

At the office there was, as usual, nothing to do. He sat and stared and yawned. Suddenly he reached a decision. He rang a friend of his at the War Office and set in motion a search of the regimental records of Alban's unit. Within a few hours, and after some expensive phone calls which could be explained away or paid for later, Otford had discovered that Alban's A.D.C. at the time of the crossing of the Rizzio had been a certain Lieutenant Gilkie, who was now farming in Kenya, and that Alban's batman had been a Private Jack Lennock, who was believed to be a member of the Corps of Commissionaires. With the help of that organization, Jack Lennock was soon traced to a cinema in Leicester Square. Forgoing his lunch, Otford took a cab to Leicester Square, went up to the tall florid doorman in his resplendent operetta uniform, and asked for Lennock. The doorman revealed that Lennock worked in the offices upstairs, but that he did not come on until three o'clock.

As Otford sat in a milk bar, eating an inferior hamburger, he couldn't think why he was so impatient. All the evidence pointed to the fact that there was no mystery.

Gribbell and Alban had agreed, and Alban, the defendant, had been if anything more energetic in his protestation of guilt than Gribbell, the plaintiff. And yet, Otford's instinct told him that he was on the eve of a discovery, that the investigation must go on.

At three o'clock, Otford went into the offices of the movie company, located above the cinema, and, on the eighth floor, found Lennock seated at a desk. He was dressed in his dark uniform and wore a row of medals. When Otford approached him, he looked up and smiled. He had a pleasant, open face. 'And whom would you like to see, sir?' he asked.

'I believe it's you I'm looking for.'

'Me?'

'Mr Lennock?'

'Yes.'

Otford introduced himself and then asked point-blank about Alban.

The expression on Lennock's face changed. An ancient pain seemed to be rekindled in his eyes. 'I've been through that enough, sir,' said Lennock, 'and so's the old man, I reckon. I'd rather forget the whole thing.'

Otford offered him a pound note, which Lennock refused.

'Did you like him?'

'Me? I never saw finer. But you had to know him, of course. He had his ups and downs, like anyone else.'

'Was he rather fond of the bottle, though?'

Lennock looked at Otford with suspicion and even a little anger. 'He'd like a drink at the right time, sir, same as you would.'

'Did you take part in the crossing of the river?'

'I did, sir, yes,' said Lennock.

'Were you one of those who reached the other side?'

'We all reached the other side, sir.'

'All of you? The whole brigade?'

'The whole brigade.'

Otford frowned. 'How far did you get?'

'I'm not one to ask, sir. I was wounded in the foot as soon as we got over, and went to hospital. When I came out, I was sent to the Far East to our 8th Battalion, and I never saw any of the lads again.'

'Is there anyone you keep in touch with, anyone I could ask?'

'There's not many in London, sir, apart from Company Sergeant-Major Lambert, of "C" Company. He's in charge of the Turkish baths at the Automobile Athletic Club, down on Jermyn Street. I see him occasionally.'

Just then an employee of the film company wandered out and called Lennock.

'Excuse me a moment, sir,' he said, and went.

Otford did not wait for him to return. He left the building, hailed a taxi, and went to the Automobile Athletic Club. It was quite a business for a non-member to enter, but the fact that Otford was a member of at least one other reputable club seemed to convince the secretary, and after some quite unnecessary conversation Otford was escorted to the Turkish bath and presented to C. S. M. Lambert, a small wiry man with a sharpness about his features which would make even a serene conscience uneasy. He was dressed from head to foot in white and moved with the springy step of the physical training instructor.

Otford wasted no time in asking his questions.

'I don't know if it's my place to answer, sir, seeing as I don't have any precise knowledge as to your authority to ask them.'

'But you must have some opinions,' said Otford, who loathed the pomposity of the joyously downtrodden.

'Opinions I may have, sir, but that don't mean I have the

permission at all times to express same, if you follow my meaning.'

'No, I don't follow your meaning.' John was annoyed.

'Well, put it this way. I don't know whether what we went through at the crossing or fording of the River Rizzio is still on the secret list or not.'

'Has anyone told you it is?'

'No one has told me it isn't,' said the sergeant-major cannily, believing he had won a point. Dear god, what a fool.

'You knew Brigadier Alban?'

'Colonel Alban, sir.'

'If you insist on being ungenerous.'

'I'm being accurate, sir.'

'Was he, in your opinion, a good officer?'

'My opinions don't count, sir. What counts is one, a man's record, and two, the findings of the court martial.'

'Did you agree with the findings of the court martial?'

'It's not up to me to agree or disagree, but to act according.'

'But great heavens, man, you were there!'

'Exactly!' said the sergeant-major, with irritating emphasis.

Otford tried a fresh approach. 'You crossed the River Rizzio on the 29th November. That is common knowledge.'

'If you know it, sir, it must be.'

'I gather the entire battalion got across the river before it was brought back.'

'I can't tell you that, sir.'

'Who d'you think it's going to help if you do,' cried Otford. 'The Germans? They're on our side now, and very eager to be helpful.'

'Then why don't you ask them?'

'By Jove, that's an idea!'

The sergeant-major lost his composure. The thought that

he might have given Otford an idea was dismaying. 'What do you intend to do, sir?' he asked, his eyes narrowing melodramatically.

'I intend to take your advice and find out the truth from the Germans.'

'I never advised you to do that!'

'You did,' Otford replied. 'You said why don't I just ask them.'

'I didn't mean exactly that, sir, but if there is anything you want to know, I'd be obliged if you'd check with Major Angwin. He took over the battalion when the old man, Colonel Radford, was killed.' Now he was all anxiety and breathlessness.

'That's better,' said Otford. 'Major Angwin, did you say? D'you know where I can reach him?'

'Yes, sir. We still exchange Christmas cards, sir. He's a truck distributor now, sir, in Lincoln. Angwin Brothers is the name of the firm.'

'Thank you very much.'

Otford held out a pound note, which the company sergeant-major accepted with a little bow.

Otford reached the museum at about half-past four and found that there had been no messages and that no one had phoned. He glanced once again at the copy of *Those Were My Orders*.

'Although two companies managed to get a precarious foothold on the further bank of the river, the casualties were enormous and I was forced to bring them back,' he read again.

And yet Lennock had said that the entire brigade had crossed. Perhaps Lennock wasn't in a position to know. Perhaps Gribbell wasn't either?

Otford found the number of Angwin Brothers in Lincoln

quite easily, and soon he was talking to Major Angwin on the long-distance line. Judging by his voice, Angwin fancied himself as a born leader of both men and trucks.

'Alban?' he said. 'I detested the fellow, ill-mannered as they come, vain as hell, and eccentric to boot. Used to wear his cap back to front and take a parade in pyjamas. You know the type of thing. Regular show-off. Mind you, I'll say this for him, the men would follow him anywhere. He had a kind of magic. He made them laugh. They thought he was mad, and there certainly wasn't a dull moment when he was around but when you got him in the officers' mess, he was a real menace.'

'Did he drink?'

'Yes, but he held his liquor remarkably well. I've never known a fellow could hold his drink the way he did. Incredible. And I never saw him lose his lucidity.'

'Did you ever come across Sir Crowdson Gribbell?'

'Yes, another perfectly vile fellow. Poles apart from wild man Alban, of course, a real Colonel Blimp. Never took a risk in his life. Never advanced an inch unless he was sure of success, and until the divisions on his flanks had done all the dirty work. At least Alban kept you awake, but a conversation with Yawner Gribbell had you snoring in no time.'

Refreshing, this man Angwin.

'General Gribbell's written a book.'

'The Yawn? Glad I haven't any money in it. What's he say?'

'He says that when Alban launched his attack, only two companies got across, and—'

'That's a complete and utter lie. My battalion was in reserve, and we got across behind the two other battalions of the brigade.'

'He says the foothold was precarious.'

'Would you believe it? The aim of the exercise was to try and reach the village of San something or other—'

'San Melcchore di Stetto.'

'That's it. Well, we occupied the place in less than half an hour after the attack started. Casualties were very light. Alban began digging in and sent a message back, asking for divisional support. The only answer he got was an order to retreat. He refused at first but had to give in in the end. There was practically a mutiny when the men found themselves retreating for no reason. That move of ours gave Jerry confidence, and he opened up a murderous fire. Ninety-five per cent of our casualties were suffered during the retreat.'

'Good god.'

'Yes, well, there it is, for what it's worth. Anytime you're in Lincoln . . .'

Feverishly Otford called the War Office again and found out from his contacts there that the German general opposing Gribbell's division had been a certain General Schwantz, who was, as luck would have it, still on the active list and attached to the North Atlantic Treaty Forces in Paris. Although it was getting late, Otford placed a call to Paris and found that General Schwantz was not at headquarters but could be reached at the Hotel Raphael. Glancing anxiously at his watch, he placed a call to the Raphael, only to find that General Schwantz was out, probably at a reception at the German Embassy, honouring some visiting American leader. Relentless, Otford phoned the German Embassy, and, mustering the few words of German at his disposal, he asked for General Schwantz. Someone at the other end went to look for him, and Otford could hear the muffled roar of cocktail voices. Otford reflected that he could do with a drink. Eventually a voice came on the line and said in rather high, soft tones, 'Hallo, hier Schwantz.'

'Do you speak English?'

'Who is on the apparatus?'

Otford explained that he was a military historian and apologized for bothering the general at such a time. Since the Germans have a great respect for historians of any kind, especially military ones, the general was more than courteous.

'I want to ask you a question about the crossing of the River Rizzio, sir.'

'Rizzio? Yes. Perhaps I send you my book, *Sonnenuntergang in Italien.* Is here difficult to talk because is much noise.'

'You've written a book?'

'Yes. For two weeks it appeared in Munich, in German of course. I send it to you.'

'Thank you very much indeed, sir. I shall read it with pleasure. May I just ask you one more question, though?'

'Please.'

'Did the 29th November attack take you by surprise?'

'Completely. There was no artillery preparation. We were accustomed to the English always attacking in the same way. Artillery and then, after one hour or so, infantry. Here was something quite different. The attack was led by an officer in white. What he was wearing looked like pyjamas. He was smoking a pipe and holding one Union Jack in his hand. Many of the soldiers were smoking, too, and playing pipes and bugles and hitting drums. It was a form of attack we used during World War I called a psychological attack, and in this case the morale of my soldiers was so low, they abandoned their positions often without firing. They had come from Russia, you see, and the General Staff considered Italy like a holiday after Russia, but of course it was as bad, only smaller. Some of the soldiers were so nervous, they thought this white figure was a ghost, or a, how you say, corpse. The strange cacophony, all this was very clever, the cleverest thing I have ever seen in war, because the psychological moment was chosen for doing it. In 1914 to 1918, we lost many men by doing it when the enemy was fresh and his morale was high. I was unable to save our headquarters in the village of San Melcchore di Stetto, and our line was broken. One of my last actions was to send an urgent message asking for help to the corps commander, General Von Hammerlinck, but I knew that Von Hammerlinck would have to order a general retreat, because we had no reserves at this time. I had under my command small elements of the 381st Division, two hundred men perhaps, about five hundred of the Grosser Kurfürst Grenadiers, some over-age soldiers of various holding units, and about three hundred fanatics from the SS Division Seyss-Inquart. I mixed them as much as was possible, because if prisoners should be taken I wished to give the impression to the British that we were strong. I had already ordered a local retreat in order to prevent a complete collapse of morale – some of our soldiers had been in the line without relief for eight, nine months – when for some reason which was never explained the British themselves retreated. When the message was brought to me, I did not believe it, but I ordered a full attack. When soldiers are tired and morale is low, they must have activity. Even a hopeless charge is better than nothing. Within two hours we had returned to our original positions, and we inflicted severe casualties on the enemy. I was awarded the Ritterkreuz with diamonds, but I admit in my memoirs that I did not deserve this. Never in my military career have I known such an extraordinary and even mysterious mistake as the British made on that occasion. Does this answer your question?'

The Germans are nothing if not thorough. For a man

who had begged to be excused because of the difficulty of talking within earshot of a cocktail party, General Schwantz had certainly done his subject proud.

'Thank you very much, Herr General,' said Otford, 'you've given me more than enough information, and I will take the liberty of sending you a book to read.'

'Please?'

The general talked almost perfect English when he was recounting a military exploit, but in conversation he was not so happy.

'Thank you very much,' said Otford.

'Thank you, and best wishes with your very interesting work.'

Otford hung up and smiled grimly.

He called Philip Hedges and told him there might be a slight alteration to be inserted into the new version of the encyclopedia. Hedges was delighted. Then Otford went to the florist, bought a large bouquet of red roses, and drove home.

His wife was weary of the oppressive silence of a family dispute which only had a degree of thoughtlessness at its base and no sinister intentions. The gift of roses made her cry, since the gesture was so unlike her husband, and in bed that night he told her the whole story.

'I somehow couldn't tell you before,' he said, 'since it wasn't clear in my own mind.'

'I understand,' she whispered, although she really didn't.

He looked at her out of the corner of his eye and grinned. 'I'll need your help tomorrow, though. We're going out to see Colonel Alban in the morning.'

'You need my help?' She was flattered.

'Yes, indeed,' he said. 'If I went alone, he might be tempted to knock me down. In front of a lady, I hope he won't dare.'

\* \* \*

The next morning, the Otfords motored out to Sunningdale. They arrived at the colonel's shack at about half-past eleven. In daylight, it looked considerably humbler than it had looked at night. It was made of corrugated iron, its bleakness somewhat disguised by vines and other creepers. Only the tiny garden was remarkable for its tidiness. Otford rang the doorbell. After a pause, Mrs Alban opened the door.

She seemed horrified to see Otford.

'Who is it?' a gruff voice called from the interior of the house.

She did not dare answer, but just hovered uncomfortably.

The colonel appeared, a dead pipe reversed in his mouth. He was wearing shorts and a thick grey pullover.

'What the hell d'you want?' he said abruptly. 'I thought I showed you the door last time you came.'

'You didn't show me the door,' answered Otford gamely. 'You didn't even ask me in. This is my wife, Jean.'

Alban nodded curtly, his brown eyes moving uncertainly from one to the other.

'Hadn't they better come in?' Mrs Alban ventured timidly.

'No. What d'you want?'

'I know the truth about the crossing of the River Rizzio, and I intend to publish it.'

'There's no truth about it which isn't generally known.'

'That's not Private Lennock's opinion.'

'Private Lennock? Where did you dig him up?'

'Never mind.'

'He's not qualified to say what happened.'

'What about C.S.M. Lambert and Major Angwin?'

'Lambert's the worst type of regular soldier, a time-server. As for Angwin, he's a headstrong fool, an amateur aping the professionals. Anything they might state, I would deny.'

'How about General Schwantz?'

'General Schwantz?'

Colonel Alban smiled slightly, the smile of one who recognizes a point gained by an opponent.

'Come in,' he said. 'Madge, look after Mrs Otford, will you? I want to talk to Mr Otford alone. In my study.'

Jean looked at her husband, who nodded encouragingly.

'I'd like to show you some of the jams I've been making,' said Mrs Alban.

Jean followed her with a singular lack of enthusiasm. It was a man's world.

Otford followed the colonel.

'Now, before you say anything,' said Alban, 'd'you notice anything about this room?'

'Well, I notice a fantastic, a tremendous collection of plants. A regiment of plants, one might almost say.'

The colonel's voice became hard again. 'I will allow any collective noun but that.'

'Some of these are Oriental, aren't they?'

'Yes,' said the colonel, 'that little fellow's Tibetan, this rather ugly blighter's from Kashmir, they're from all over the world. Very tricky, they are, too. Have to be kept at different temperatures under glass, and it isn't easy in a private house. Still, with a little ingenuity, almost anything can be done.' He smiled. 'As you have proved.'

'How long have you been doing this?' Otford asked.

'Ever since I left the Army. You notice nothing else? Of a negative nature perhaps?'

Otford looked around the room in silence, searching for clues.

'It's nothing detailed,' Alban went on. 'Have you ever been in the room of a military man?'

Suddenly it struck Otford. 'There's not a single photograph of a regimental reunion,' he said, 'not a single relic, no framed portraits of field-marshals.'

'Exactly,' Alban replied. 'Now you have put me at ease. Scotch? It's all I have.'

'Isn't it a little early?'

'Never too early for Scotch.'

Alban poured out two neat ones and gave a glass to Otford.

'Could I have a little—'

'Water spoils it,' said Alban. 'Now.'

He sat down on a camp stool, leaving a broken armchair for Otford.

'I want to clear something up,' Otford said. 'Why were you so abrupt in manner until I mentioned Schwantz's name? And why are you so hospitable now?'

The colonel laughed and scratched his cheek with a nico-tined finger. He filled his pipe slowly while thinking how to answer. 'There's nothing on earth I admire more than in-telligence. I admire people who know when to obey their instincts. That's part of intelligence too. You must have done that. You proved to me that you weren't just a fool out for a sensational story, you were a man who smelled a rat and used your head smelling it out. I did everything to discourage you the other night. I put you off the scent, and you came right back on it. I admire that, and it made you worthy of my hospitality.' The man was certainly a leader by temperament. He was so serene in his vanity that it was impossible to take offence. He lit his pipe slowly.

'You think you're going to get a story out of me,' he went on. 'You're not. The most I can do for you is to make you comfortable for a moment.'

'You're not even eager to know what Schwantz said?' Otford asked.

'No. He undoubtedly told the truth. I wish he hadn't.'

'You're content to let Gribbell's version of the story go unchallenged?'

'Oh, yes.' Alban was almost negligent in his reply. He

looked up, saw Otford's puzzled face, and laughed aloud. 'I was spoiled by my superiors. I was a kind of overgrown boy scout really, and that's what the Army approved of in those days. The Balkan campaign at the end of World War I was real fun, full of intolerant French officers, Serbs on their dignity, Bulgarians with hurt national feelings, and Greek merchants making a lot of money with delightful impertinence. Estonia was fun too, raiding the Bolshevik lines, capturing women soldiers – I felt as Byron must have felt in Greece. Archangel was too cold for comfort, but the week-ends I had spent in English country houses were admirable training for it, and I managed to enjoy it. Later on, in India, I played a great deal of polo really well and consequently got rapid promotion. People were killed all the time, of course, but I was younger, and it seemed to be the luck of the game.'

He paused for a moment and stared at the smoke from his pipe. 'The rot began to set in when I got to France in '39. It seemed to me that I was surrounded by the biggest bunch of jackasses I had ever seen together at the same time. Their stupidity was so crushing that it was consistently entertaining. The men spent their time polishing their buttons and rushing at sacks with their bayonets, screaming so loud they frightened themselves. All the training seemed to be directed towards making the men as conspicuous as possible. I beefed and complained to no avail. When Jerry made his big push, we did what we could to facilitate his task, and we can flatter ourselves we lost even more convincingly than he won.

'After that, Ethiopia was like a reversion to the kind of wars I had enjoyed. Not much killing, just a lot of extremely beautiful scenery, and a healthy life out in the open. Then London, the hothouse, desk work galore, throwing bits of vaguely worded papers from tray to tray. I was beginning to tire of it all, when they sent me out to give

old Crowdy Gribbell a helping hand. He was horrified
when he saw me again after all those years, and he hadn't
the character to insist that I go. Not much character,
Crowdy. I'm being overgenerous. No character. We sat on
the south bank of that lousy stream with the pretty name –
the troops called it the Ritzy – for a full two months, doing
nothing but waiting for the enemy to retreat.

'I knew perfectly well Jerry was putting on a big act.
There was far too much movement on his bank of the river
for it not to be just for show, but it took old Crowdy in. He
was in mortal terror of a Hun attack. Then they called him
up to H.Q. and put him on the mat. He came back white
with anger. He was always very easily hurt, old Crowdy,
usually because he didn't quite understand what was being
said to him, and he wanted to be on the safe side. He asked
some of us to dine with him. Bloody awful dinner, I remember. Bloody by any standards. He asked for our support in his determination not to stick his neck out by
attacking. "Damned if I'll show my hand before the Boche
does," he said. I lost my temper and told him I was
ashamed to be serving with him and a lot of other things
rather less temperate. I always overdid it a bit, chiefly because he wouldn't have understood it otherwise. I stalked
off to my brigade H.Q. and planned to use one of Jerry's
oldest tricks on Jerry himself. Just after dawn, "A" Company went forward on a very narrow front, banging tin
trays, smoking, faces blacked, some of them in underwear,
others carrying sheets tied to their rifles. I led the charge in
pyjamas, smoking a pipe and reading a copy of the *Illus-
trated London News* as I walked. We made as much noise
as we could. One fellow had some bagpipes, there were
four buglers, three harmonicas, a mouth organ or two, and
a hell of a lot of shouting. We went through the Hun like a
knife through butter and marched into San Melcchore di
Stetto half an hour later.'

'What were your casualties?'

'One killed, four wounded. Then I made my fatal mistake. Instead of appealing to the Polish commander on my flank for support, I sent the message to Crowdy. He replied that I was under arrest and ordered our immediate retreat, declaring that I had ruined his overall plan for seizing San Melcchore. I replied that since San Melcchore was now in our hands, there was no further need of an overall plan. This only made matters worse. He sent word that I was a liar, and the last order I obeyed in the Army was a criminal retreat. We lost four hundred and twenty-four men in that withdrawal. There.'

He frowned in anguish, then smiled again.

'I have done precisely what I said I wasn't going to. I have told you my story. D'you know why I decided to do it?'

'No.'

'Because I'm a good judge of character. That was the price I was willing to pay in order to induce you to keep quiet about this.'

'You mean you don't want me to correct the record?' Otford almost shouted.

'The record? What's the record?' Alban poured himself another drink. 'At every board meeting or meeting of Parliament they go to endless lengths to keep the record straight, and then no one ever looks at it again.'

'Unless there's a lawsuit.'

'A lawsuit needs a plaintiff. In this case, there isn't one.' Alban fixed Otford with a penetrating stare and drew his camp stool closer to the armchair.

'I wonder whether you can understand this,' he said, very quietly, almost reverently. 'I've always wanted children, and we never had any, and nothing makes you more respectful of life than the desire to give life, linked to the inability to do so. I realize certain things have to be done in the world, and there are certain talents which have to be obeyed. I was a good soldier. I don't know whether you've ever watched a game of lawn tennis. There are moments when the ball lingers on the net, undecided as to which way to fall. There are soldiers like that, and I was one of them. Either they become great military leaders, or they're cashiered because they behave like great military leaders when they haven't the rank to get away with it. That was me. I had a gift for soldiering – it might have been called genius if I'd been a bit more patient – but at heart I don't think I cared enough about the glamour when I was no longer a front-line soldier, and I began to care too much about the men when I was no longer allowed to be among them. What finally did it was that retreat, that damn, stupid, criminal retreat from the village. We lost four hundred and twenty-four men. I saw them dropping around me like flies. I hoped a bullet would get me in the small of the back as I walked back to our lines. It was what I deserved for being cowardly enough to obey Crowdy's pigheaded orders instead of sitting it out in the village until someone with a grain of sense in his head and adequate brass on his hat realized the importance of our victory. But by then, you know, I was eager to give up. Those four hundred and twenty-four casualties weren't just four hundred and twenty-four lives thrown down the drain, four hundred and twenty-four embryos, four hundred and twenty-four names on a sheet of paper, they were four hundred and twenty-four educations, four hundred and twenty-four intelligences, four hundred and twenty-four sensibilities, four hundred and twenty-four characters, four hundred and twenty-four ways of thought, and the regret of eight hundred and forty-eight parents. They died because Crowdy Gribbell was annoyed with me, for no other reason.'

'Doesn't that prove my point?' said Otford, hotly. 'Gribbell's comportment was utterly atrocious, and you were

forced to take the blame for a crime committed by someone
who has taken all the credit for the subsequent victory!'

'Is that the way you see it?' asked Alban quietly. 'I don't
agree with you, because frankly I don't care. I can't allow
you to stir up all those dormant sorrows in the hearts of the
parents of these boys by making them realise that these
deaths could have been avoided. I would rather take the
blame. And d'you know why? Because I've shoulders
broad enough to carry the burden; Crowdy hasn't. For me,
it's a closed chapter; for him, it isn't. He'll spend the rest
of his life trying to justify his action, fearful lest the controversy should reopen. I've got my plants, Otford, and I
don't care. It's splendid to see something growing, a fraction of a leaf more a day, breaking the soil, reaching for
the light, breathing. It's a compromise, but it's satisfying,
beautifully, thrillingly satisfying. I'm tired of death, and
mud, and tears, and the decisions which lead to them. I'm
a happy man. Crowdy isn't. He sits in that depressing club
he frequents and wonders what's going to happen next. He
can't take it. I can. I've less on my conscience.'

'You want me to forget the whole thing,' said Otford
slowly.

'Yes, I do. I want you to promise me to forget it.'

'General Schwantz has written a book.'

'Who's going to read it? Who's going to read Crowdy's,
for that matter? And who's going to read your articles?
Only friends, enemies, and a few students. We're not
terribly important, you and I, in the span of history. Are
you going to forget it?'

'Well—' Otford was loath to commit himself, even
though he was deeply stirred by the tranquillity of Alban's
spirit.

'I'll tell you something else about Crowdy,' said the
colonel. 'His wife died a year ago, and his only boy was
killed in France, in the last week of the war. He never

knew much about love, so that all he feels now is an emptiness, a sense of being cheated. He's stupid enough to be bitter. Well, you can't be angry for long with a poor empty shell like that.'

He poured himself a third whisky.

'I've read articles by you,' he said. 'You write well, with a crisp, malicious style. You're a good bit younger than I am, but one day you'll suddenly realize that there's more in everyone than meets the eye, you'll add a dash of pity to your writing, and then you'll begin to grow, like those plants. Have you children?'

'No,' said Otford, glumly.

'There's no . . . no reason why you can't have, is there?'

'No. I suppose we've just never got round to it.'

'Good God!' Alban exploded. 'You don't know what you're missing!'

'Do you?'

'No one knows better than a parent without children,' said Alban stoutly, with a smile. 'And now I know we understand each other, and that you will conveniently forget everything but my insubordination. Soldiers are children who never grow up, Otford. I'm growing up. Give me a chance. And incidentally, grow up yourself, before it's too late and they find a permanent armchair for you in that crèche for second childhood in St James's Street, where the old babies go to die.'

As they walked to the door, Alban added, 'Incidentally, I didn't hit my wife the other night. I never do. I was putting on an act for your benefit. She's a wonderful girl, Madge, but she cares, as you seem to, and she can never forgive me for no longer caring.'

'I can't really forgive you for that either,' said Otford, smiling awkwardly.

Otford hardly talked in the car, and since Jean had had a miserable time indulging in small talk with Mrs Alban, a stormy atmosphere began to gather again in the silence.

'Where are you going?' Jean said suddenly.

'I've something to do in town,' Otford answered curtly.

'Then drop me off home first.'

'It won't take long.'

They didn't talk again until they reached St James's Street, but Jean could tell from her husband's aggressive driving that he was upset. 'If the police come, tell them I'll be out in a moment,' he said, as he parked the car.

He ran up the steps three at a time and walked briskly into the murmuring caverns of his club. General Sir Crowdson Gribbell sat in his usual chair, staring at nothing. Otford gazed at him in cold fury. The general always carried his head at a strange angle, tilted slightly upwards, as though wondering whether an invisible fly would attempt to land on him. He expressed very little otherwise, apart from vague determination and a grey kind of breeding. Occasionally he blinked, and his white eyelashes caught the sunlight. Nobody sat near him. He was alone.

An old waiter entered, with a quarter bottle of champagne, and placed it on the low table before the general.

'Celebrating, sir?' the waiter asked as he pulled the cork and poured the wine into the glass.

'Yes,' answered the general tonelessly, 'my son's birthday.'

Otford felt a sudden lump in his throat and fled the club.

As he approached his car, he saw his wife sitting inside. She was pretty, but she had aged a little. Or perhaps her expression was just sadder than it had once been, her lips more compressed, her eyes less merry.

He got into the driver's seat and smiled at her. 'Darling,' he said, 'I want to know you better.' She laughed, not happily. 'What on earth are you talking about?' He looked at her as though seeing her for the first time, and kissed her as if they were not yet married.

Later in the day, John wrote Hedges that there would be no alterations in the article, and a few days later, when General Schwantz's book arrived, John even forgot to open the package.

# THE MAN IN THE MOON

John Kermidge walked down the street in Highgate to the letter-box, a bulky package in his hand. He felt as though he had been plunged backwards into another, more ample century, when the legs of men were still in constant use as a means of propulsion, not just as members groping for brake and accelerator. He smiled at the sky as though greeting a half-forgotten friend. There was a trace of troubled conscience in his smile. He had kept the sky waiting for so long. Usually, when he looked up, he saw nothing but the perpetual night of his laboratory.

Since he was a scientist, it would have been inhuman if he had not in some measure surrendered to tradition and been a little absent-minded. Not in his work, but in relatively unimportant matters. When he wrote, he did so with vast application, and the meaning of his words could only be fathomed by a few dozen endowed creatures in various universities; but often, as now, having filled pages with mysterious logic, he forgot to stick any stamps to the envelope. The letter was addressed to Switzerland, to a Doctor Nussli, in Zurich. Considering that Dr Nussli was perhaps John's best friend, it was strange, if typical, that the name on the envelope was spelled with a single *s*.

'Where did you go?' asked his wife anxiously when he returned.

'I posted that letter to Hans.'

'Couldn't it have waited until the morning?'

Although the weather was cold, John mopped his brow with his handkerchief. 'No,' he said.

'The last mail's gone anyway,' Veronica grumbled.

It was curious that John should feel irritated in his hour of triumph, but he allowed himself a moment of harshness.

'No,' he repeated, unnecessarily loud.

There was a pause, with thunder in the air.

For quite a few months, Veronica and John had seen very little of each other. Veronica had permitted herself quite a few questions during this time; John had failed to gratify her with even a single answer.

'I thought you might like to see the children before they went to bed,' she said.

He grunted and asked, 'Where's Bill?'

'Bill? I don't know. Sir Humphrey called.'

'Sir Humphrey?' John started angrily. 'What the hell did he want?'

'He didn't say, but he was unusually nice to me.'

'That's a bad sign.'

'Seemed very elated.'

'Elated?' John kicked a chair.

'What's the matter with you?' Veronica almost shouted.

The doorbell rang.

'That'll be the champagne,' John said, going into the entrance hall.

'Champagne?'

It wasn't the champagne. It was Bill Hensey, John's assistant, a bearded fellow in an old sports jacket, with a dead pipe permanently in his mouth. He seized John by the arm, didn't even acknowledge Veronica, and started speaking agitatedly in a soft voice. Veronica wished she'd married a bank clerk, a man with simple problems and a little courtesy. She heard nothing of the conversation apart from an occasional reference to Sir Humphrey, but she saw Bill's baleful blue eyes darting hither and thither with excitement.

She was a pleasant girl without much temperament, the ideal wife for John, if there was such a thing. She didn't wish to attract attention to herself, since she knew that both men were engaged in important work and that they were under some strain which it was her unhappy duty to understand without being inquisitive. Just then, however, the children burst into the room, engaged in a running fight over the cactus-covered plains of the frontier badlands. Dick, dressed as a sheriff over his pyjamas, opened murderous fire with a cap pistol from behind an armchair, while Timothy plunged into cover behind the radiogram, his eyes shining evilly through the slits of his bandit's mask.

John exploded. 'Get out of here,' he yelled.

It was only natural for Veronica to leap to her children's defence. 'They're only playing,' she cried. 'God Almighty, what's the matter with you?'

'Can't you see we're working?' answered John, covering up his guilt in testiness.

But Veronica was roused, and launched into a big scene. While the children slunk out unhappily, she released all her resentment in a flood of tears and invective. She had been packing for this blasted trip to Washington. Did he think she wanted to go to Washington? She'd much rather stay home. Why didn't he go alone? And if he went, why didn't he stay? What thanks did she get? To her the unglamorous lot: the paying of bills, the checking of accounts, the necessary bedtime stories which taxed the imagination. Why didn't he marry Bill?

She was interrupted by the doorbell. The champagne, no doubt.

It wasn't the champagne. It was Sir Humphrey Utteridge, accompanied by an affected youth in a bowler hat.

'Kermidge, allow me to congratulate you,' Sir Humphrey said in a voice that was quivering with emotion.

John and Bill exchanged a quick, anxious look.

'Thank you, Sir Humphrey,' John answered, with some impatience.

'This event will mark the beginning of a new era, not only in the annals of recorded history, but in the indelible odyssey of the British Commonwealth of Nations.'

This was the fine, rolling language for launching a ship, but nobody wants a ship launched in his living-room.

'Old ass,' thought John, but said, 'It's very good of you to say so.'

'D'you remember me, Kermidge?' asked the affected youth, leaning heavily on his umbrella. 'Oliver de Vouvenay. We were at Charterhouse together.'

Good gracious. No wonder John didn't remember him, he hadn't changed a bit. John's hair was turning white, but this immaculate, pink creature looked exactly as he had at school. If he was now successful, it was a triumph of conformity. He was successful.

After John had grudgingly shaken hands, Oliver de Vouvenay announced that he hadn't done badly, since he was now the Principal Private Secretary of the Prime Minister, the Right Honourable Arthur Backworth, and hoped to stand in the next election.

'Not as a Socialist,' said John.

Oliver de Vouvenay laughed uproariously and expressed his conviction that the joke was a good one.

Before there was time for more banter, the doorbell rang again.

'That'll be—' Sir Humphrey began, but John interrupted him.

'I ordered some champagne,' he said. 'I'll go.'

John opened the door and found himself face to face with a detective. The man didn't say he was a detective, but it was obvious. His disguise would only have deceived another detective. 'This is it, sir,' called the detective to a waiting Rolls-Royce.

The door of the limousine opened slowly, and an elderly

man of some distinction struggled cautiously on to the pavement.

John felt the colour draining from his face. He recognized the man as the Right Honourable Arthur Backworth, Prime Minister of Great Britain and Northern Ireland.

'May I come in?' said the Prime Minister, with a vote-catching smile.

Here was a wonderful, perverse moment to say no, but John said yes.

Veronica, amazed, and with an intense feeling of shame at having even mentioned such trivialities as accounts and packing, watched her humble suburban boudoir gradually filling with celebrities who had only graced it previously as guests on the television screen.

'You will probably wonder why I am here,' crooned Mr Backworth.

Once again John was seized with a desire to say no, but to the Prime Minister the question was a rhetorical one, and he continued in august and measured tones.

'When Sir Humphrey informed me early today of the success of your experiment, I immediately called a Cabinet meeting, which ended not half an hour ago. It goes without saying that what you have achieved is perhaps the most glorious, the most decisive step forward in the history of science – nay, of the human race. What recognition a mere government may accord you will be yours, rest assured.'

'It would have been impossible without Bill here—' John said.

'Yes, yes, both of you, both of you,' the Prime Minister went on with some impatience. He was used to the interruptions of politicians, but the interruptions of laymen were an impertinence. 'Now, it must be obvious to you,' he continued, 'that what you have accomplished is of such magnitude that it cannot fail to affect the policy of nations, and,' he added, with a trace of exalted mischief, 'of this nation in particular. After all, the Russians will, at any moment, be able to land a dog on the moon; the Americans have, I am told, a mouse in readiness; but we, without fanfares or magniloquence, have by-passed these intermediary stages and are ready to land a man, or men. You may not realize what this means.'

John smiled and said modestly, 'I am very fortunate, sir, that it should have fallen to me to head the team which managed, perhaps more by luck than by virtue, to achieve this success. I am, of course, looking forward immensely to my visit to Washington, and to the possibility of breaking this news to our American friends.' John was slightly annoyed with himself for adopting this formal tone, but in talking to Prime Ministers one apparently didn't talk, one made a speech.

Mr Backworth looked at John curiously, and smiled. 'I want you to come to dinner on Thursday at Number 10,' he said.

'I can't, I'll be in Washington.'

'No, you won't.'

'What?'

The Prime Minister nodded at Sir Humphrey, who cleared his throat and spoke. 'It has been decided by the Cabinet – and I was present at the meeting – to send Gwatkin-Pollock to Washington in your place. We need you here.'

'But Gwatkin-Pollock knows not the first thing about interplanetary travel!' John cried.

'Then he will give nothing away,' said the Prime Minister, pleasantly.

'This is outrageous. I want to go!'

'You can't,' replied the Prime Minister.

'Can't!' echoed John, and then fell back on the conventional reaction of the perplexed democrat. 'This is a free country.'

'Yes,' growled the Prime Minister, in his heroic style, 'and we must keep it free.'

His remark didn't mean much, but any student of politics will recognize the fact that it is more important to make the right noise than to talk sense.

The Prime Minister smiled, relaxing the unexpected tension. 'Do you really think that we have sunk so low as to reward you by curbing your liberties?' he asked.

John felt childish. 'I was looking forward to Washington,' he said.

'You scientists take such a long view of events that it needs simple souls like ourselves to open your eyes to the obvious on occasion. Of course you are flushed with pride of achievement. Of course you wish to announce your world-shattering discovery to your colleagues. That is only human. But alas! Your colleagues may be near to you in spirit, but they also carry passports, they also speak their various languages and boast their various prejudices. There can be no pure relationship between you and, say, a Russian scientist, because you both have divergent responsibilities, however warm and cordial your contact in your laboratories or over a cup of coffee. Now, you harbour a tremendous, a dangerous secret. Have you the experience to keep it, all by yourself, without help from us? Will not the strain on you be utterly inhuman, however loyal your intentions? These are questions to which we must find answers within the next few weeks.'

'How do you intend to go about it?' asked John, too surprised to be really angry.

'By keeping your mind occupied,' said the Prime Minister, earnestly. 'Thursday is the day after tomorrow. I wish you to dine with me and with General Sir Godfrey Toplett, Chief of the General Staff.'

'We will have absolutely nothing in common,' said John.

'Before dinner, perhaps not. After dinner, I believe you will,' replied the Prime Minister coolly.

'I presume that I may go on seeing which friends I please?' asked John, his voice charged with irony.

The Prime Minister ignored the irony and said, 'Up to a point.'

John looked at Oliver de Vouvenay, who smiled fatuously.

Bill rose from his seat. He hadn't said anything, but was visibly dismayed. 'If you'll excuse me . . .' he began.

'Don't be alarmed if you should feel yourself followed,' said the Prime Minister. 'You will be.'

Gwatkin-Pollock was a man of science often selected by the British Government for official missions, since he had a quality of aloof and calculating majesty which those seated with him round a conference table never failed to find disturbing. He always seemed to be hiding something. He also had a habit of suddenly, unreasonably laughing at a comic situation of a day, a week, a year ago, usually while a serious statement was being read by someone else. His enigmatic quality was completed by his utter silence when it was his turn to make a statement.

It so happened that at the very moment Gwatkin-Pollock was seated with American scientists at a top-level conference in Washington, John was puffing one of the Prime Minister's better cigars and rather losing his critical sense in its lullaby of fumes. The dark plans of the British Government were working well for the time being on both fronts. A brilliant American scientist, who spoke for some reason with a thick German accent, was just expounding a remarkable plan for projecting a whole battalion of white mice into space, when Gwatkin-Pollock, remembering a humorous event from his youth, laughed loudly. The American delegation looked at each other with consternation and asked themselves whether the President had been wise to let the British into these top-secret conferences.

In London, meanwhile, General Toplett, a soldier with a face like a whiskered walnut, was busy producing some large photographs from his portfolio.

'You see,' he said to John and to the Prime Minister, 'it's quite clear that whatever nation is the first to land even light forces on Crater K here – I've marked it in red – will control all the lateral valleys on this side of the moon's face. My plan, therefore, is to land light airborne forces as near the perimeter of the crater as possible, and to advance from there in four columns until we reach this green line here.'

This was too much for John, who leaped to his feet. 'It's revolting!' he cried. 'I didn't evolve a man-carrying moon rocket in order to see it subjected to the kind of thought which has made such a mess of our planet! I don't want dim soldiers and soiled politicians to pollute my moon!'

'Steady there, steady,' snarled the general, holding the photograph of the crater in the air as though it were a hand grenade.

The Prime Minister laughed. 'Don't you think, Kermidge,' he said quietly, 'that there is a pleasant irony in this turn of events? Don't misunderstand me; the Americans are, and always will be, our allies. That goes without saying. But in a way, we do have a . . . a friendly score to settle, don't you think?'

'In the world of science there is always an element of quite innocuous rivalry—' John said, as reasonably as he could.

'I wasn't referring to the world of science,' the Prime Minister interrupted. 'I was referring to history. Kermidge, we are taxing our ingenuity to the limit to keep over fifty million people fully employed and well fed on this tiny island. Naturally our rules are stringent, our taxation inhuman, and naturally we tend to appear to other nations as somewhat avaricious in our methods and as almost ludicrously inflexible in our regulations. Can this give us pleasure? We, who gave the world so much?'

'We took quite a lot, too,' said John.

'I must ask you to listen to me without interruption,' replied the Prime Minister with a trace of irritation. He had to put up with this kind of thing from the opposition all the year round. There was no reason, he felt, why he should put up with contradiction in his own dining-room, in his own cigar smoke. 'The Americans are a most generous people,' he continued, 'but they can afford to be. A man with one hundred pounds in the bank giving a penny to a beggar is making the same financial sacrifice as a man with one million pounds in the bank giving four pounds, three shillings, and fourpence to a beggar.' These statistics were so glib that they obviously formed a staple argument of the Prime Minister's.

'The widow's mite,' said John.

The Prime Minister gave him a withering look, which dissolved rapidly into a winning smile. Politics taught a man self-control as no other profession.

'Call it what you will, the facts are clear. We need space. We need to expand, not only in order to survive, but in order to conserve our national character, our even temper, our serenity.'

'Even Hitler thought of better reasons than that,' John heard himself saying.

The Prime Minister was unruffled.

'Would we ever attack our neighbours to achieve this end? Never. But' – and he leaned forward, searchingly – 'once there is space, who knows? We've never shied at adventure. And think of it – rolling acres on the moon, or on other planets. Untold mineral wealth. Kermidge, we are in the shoes of Columbus, with the added proof of the unknown continent's existence. Look out of the window. You will see it. And we have the ship to get us there.'

'You want to paint the moon red,' murmured John. 'You want a moon worthy of Kipling, on which the sun never sets.'

'Rather well put,' said the general, now that the conversation had taken an understandable turn.

'Exactly – and why not?' cried the Prime Minister. 'Nothing in history is final. History is like the sea, constantly changing, a patchwork of phases, a mosaic of impermanent achievements. We were an occupied people once. The Saxons, the Danes, and the Romans had their will of us. Then we rose, with the determination of underdogs, and conquered the greatest empire the world has ever known. Times changed, and with them the conception of Empire. Whether we like it or not, we now live in an Era of Liberality, in which every tin-pot republic has its own voice in the United Nations. We, in our great wisdom and experience, must sit silently by while Guatemala lays claim to British Honduras. This kind of thing taxes our dignity to the uttermost, but need it last? Must we accept the defeat of Burgoyne as final? We say we lose every battle but the last. Has the last battle been fought?' He dropped his voice from a rhetorical level into the intimacy of sincerity. 'Please understand me, I do not advocate war, least of all war with America. That would be unthinkable and stupid. In any event, we would lose it. However, I, for one, do not accept Burgoyne's defeat as the end of a story.'

'Burgoyne was a fool,' said the general gratuitously.

'Let us reach the moon first. This would not only give us the space we need, it would also give us the enormous moral ascendancy necessary to resume the leadership of the free world. There can be no doubt whatever that Russia is working rapidly towards the results you have so brilliantly attained. She is, as it were, breathing down our neck.

Sharing our information with the Americans would only waste valuable weeks at this juncture, and by the time we had put our mutual scheme into operation, the Americans would be taking all the credit. They are too flushed with their own technological efficiency to admit that anyone can achieve anything without stealing their plans. Kermidge, we have made our gesture. We have sent them Gwatkin-Pollock. Let us do the rest ourselves.'

There was a pause.

John began speaking slowly, trying hard to control his voice, which was quivering. 'I hold no brief for American scientists, or for Russian scientists, or for British scientists for that matter. I have friends and enemies in all camps, since to the true men of science there are no frontiers, only advances; there are no nations, only humanity. This may sound subversive to you, but it is true, and I will explain, as temperately as I can, why it is true, what has made it true. You, sir, talked of Columbus. In his day, men for all their culture, fine painting, architecture, humanism, the rest, were still relatively savage. Life was cheap. Death was the penalty for a slight misdemeanour, slavery the penalty for an accident of birth. And why? Because there was space to conquer, horizons full of promise. Conquest was the order of the day. The avid fingers of Britain, France, Spain, and Portugal stretched into the unknown. Then, abruptly, all was found, all was unravelled. Germany and Italy attempted to put the clock back, and behaved as everyone had once behaved, and were deemed criminal for no other reason than that they were out of date and that their internal persecutions were carried against men of culture, and white men at that, instead of against their colonial subjects. They were condemned by mankind, and rightly so, because they were hungry for glory at a time when other nations were licking their chops, sated by a meal which had lasted for centuries. And why did we all become civilized, so abruptly? Because, sir, there was nothing left to conquer, nothing left to seize without a threat of general war; there was no space left.' John mopped his brow briefly and continued. 'Now what has happened? We have become conscious of space again. Cheated of horizons down on earth, we have looked upwards, and found horizons there. What will that do to us? It will put us back to pre-Columbian days. It will be the signal for military conquest, for religious wars. There will be crusades for a Catholic moon, a Protestant moon, a Muslim moon, a Jewish moon. If there are inhabitants up there, we will persecute them mercilessly before we begin to realize their value. You can't feel any affection for a creature you have never seen before, especially if it seems ugly by our standards. The United Nations will lose all control, because its enemy is the smell of space in the nostrils of the military. Life will became cheap again, and so will glory. We will put the clock back to the days of darkness, and our growing pains in the stratosphere will be at least as painful as those we suffered here on earth. I want no part of it.'

The Prime Minister looked at him with genuine affection and offered him another cigar, which he accepted automatically, with a shaking hand.

'You are looking at the world with the eyes of a historian,' said the Prime Minister, 'but the world is not run by historians. It is a luxury we cannot afford. We can't study events from such a comfortable distance, nor can we allow ourselves to be embittered so easily by the unfortunate parallels and repetitions of history. As a historian, you are no doubt right, since you look back so far in order to look forward, but as a politician you are wrong, you are wrong as a patriot.'

'I have no ambitions as a patriot,' John answered. 'I want to be a man the world is proud of.'

'You are young,' said the Prime Minister, lighting a

match for John. 'Incidentally, the Archbishop of Canterbury has expressed an urgent desire to meet you.'

'I knew it,' cried John, 'a Church of England moon!'

When he returned home, John sat up all night writing a letter. Veronica, as she lay sleepless, heard the febrile stutter of the typewriter and an occasional angry outburst. The cabin trunks still stood half-filled in the bedroom, a measure of how disappointed John and Veronica were at not going to Washington and of their uncertainty about the future.

John didn't go to bed that night, but left the house at six-thirty to post his letter. He noticed a detective loitering on the opposite pavement, but ignored him.

There was practically no conversation between Veronica and John all day, and even the children modified their games. It was as though disaster had struck the family.

After lunch, they suffered the surprise visit of a grave Sir Humphrey, accompanied by Oliver de Vouvenay at his most petulant, and a rosy-faced inspector from Scotland Yard called Peddick.

'What may I offer you?' asked John, investing his question with sarcasm. He seemed incapable of saying anything without sarcasm these days.

'Nothing. Nothing at all,' answered Sir Humphrey.

'Perhaps we could sit down?' said de Vouvenay.

'I see nothing to prevent you,' said John.

There was a brief, awkward silence.

'Well?'

In silence, Oliver de Vouvenay opened his brief-case and produced the letter which John had posted that morning. It was open.

'What are you doing with that?' John asked hotly.

'Perhaps I should take over, sir?' It was Inspector Peddick speaking. 'Did you write this?'

'What business is it of yours?'

'It's addressed to Switzerland, sir.'

'I can explain that. It is addressed to Switzerland because I intended it to arrive in Switzerland.'

'I gather, sir, that it contains information of a highly secret nature.'

'It contains information which emanated from my brain and which I do not consider secret. And in any case, for how long has it been the practice, in this free country, for the police to intercept private letters?'

'We have authority, sir, under the Official Secrets Act.'

'Could you tell me what you find particularly secret about the information contained in this letter?'

The inspector smiled. 'That's hardly my province, sir. It doesn't make much sense to me, but I've been told it's secret from higher-up, and I acted accordingly.'

'But you've read it?'

'Oh, I skimmed through part of it, yes, sir, in the course of duty.'

John broke a vase and shouted a profanity.

Sir Humphrey raised a restraining hand. 'You must realize, John, that you must be in some measure subject to government policy. You can't go on being a rebel all your grown life. What you have accomplished is far too important to us all for you to attempt to destroy it by what you imagine to be scientific integrity. John, I implore you to regard yourself as the caretaker of a secret, and not to do anything in your moment of imminent triumph which will bring you into disrepute.'

'I am not the caretaker of a secret,' thundered John, 'I am the inventor of a public utility!'

'You wrote a letter to Switzerland, to a Professor Nussli. Professor Nussli has been to Moscow recently,' said de Vouvenay, smoothly.

'So what?' snapped John. 'I've been to Trinidad, that

doesn't mean I sing calypsos all day. What god-awful idiots you all are. Just because a man is inquisitive, just because he wants to find out, you think automatically that he's tarnished by whatever he went to investigate.'

'I didn't insinuate that at all.'

'Why did you mention it then? What do people mean when they say the word "Moscow" out of the blue? How naïve do you think I am? I've known Nussli for nearly forty years – in other words, all my life. I was brought up in Switzerland when I was young because I had asthma. I went to school with Hans. We were firm friends. He's a brilliant man now as he was a brilliant boy then, and he knows probably more about my particular field than any other man alive today. He's a thoroughly enlightened, liberal chap.'

'I'm very gratified to hear it,' said de Vouvenay.

'*You're* gratified to hear it?' shouted John, losing his temper. 'And who the hell d'you think you are? I very much regret leaving my Swiss school, where I worked and had fun, to come back here for the sole privilege of watching your nasty little career developing from the self-righteous goody-goody with the only unbroken voice in school which could do justice to the soprano solos in the *Messiah* to the pompous prig who has the impertinence to ventilate opinions about which he knows nothing, nothing, nothing! Get out of here.'

De Vouvenay rose, flushed with anger, his yellow hair falling over one eye. 'Your letter will be confiscated for the time being,' he said, 'and perhaps, in time, you will learn to behave yourself sufficiently for us to be able to entrust you with Herr Nussli's answers.'

John was aghast. 'D'you mean—'

Sir Humphrey looked at him steadily and openly. 'I will apologize for Mr de Vouvenay,' he said, 'since Mr de Vouvenay evidently hasn't the resources to apologize himself.'

'Letters to me—'

'Yes, John. I deplore the practice of opening other people's mail. Especially do I deplore it when it is perpetrated by a government. But, as an Englishman, and as one who recognized your great talent early in your life, I must say that I realize the necessity for such an emergency measure at this time. We must not only protect our secret from any enemy, but we must protect you from yourself. I don't know what you have been writing to Professor Nussli during these past months, but the one answer in our possession suggests that he has a detailed and even a brilliant insight into our methods. What is especially disturbing is his apparent knowledge of our fuel—'

'Our fuel, fiddlesticks. It was his fuel as much as mine. How do you think two friends work when they are fired by the same ambition? They share their information, selflessly, for the common good.'

'In the mail? Neither of these letters was so much as registered.'

'Surely the mail is more discreet than the telephone, and it's certainly less expensive. I never for one moment believed that my letters would be opened. Had I known that, I would have found other methods of communication.'

'Such as?' asked de Vouvenay.

'Pigeons,' spat John.

When the visitors had left, John chided himself for not having hit de Vouvenay. He had actually been forced to defend himself from a position which was as strong as any position could be in a country with democratic traditions. His correspondence had been confiscated, and yet somehow he didn't feel that he had been able to bring it home to his tormentors how unethical their conduct had been. He had certainly become very angry, but his anger had somehow been dissipated by his sheer amazement that such things were possible in this day and age, in the twentieth

century. The twentieth century? The threshold of the
second fifteenth century more likely: the age of discovery,
of casual death and roughshod life.

He made a quick decision. Lifting the telephone, he
called British European Airways and booked a flight on
the plane to Zurich. With two hours to kill, he paced the
room reconstructing the scene with his three visitors and
his dinner with the Prime Minister, his mood settling into
one of cold and righteous indignation as he thought of all
the choice phrases he would have used had he had the
presence of mind.

Then, with forty minutes to go, he put his passport in
his pocket, decided not to say good-bye to his wife, since
explanations would only dilute his fury, and left the house,
quietly closing the front door. The taxi arrived at London
Airport with some minutes to spare, and John went into
the departure hall. The young ladies were very polite and
directed him into Immigration. Here, a colourless gentleman looked at his passport for a small eternity, seeming to
read mysterious meanings into old visas. Eventually the
colourless gentleman looked up, not at John, but past him.

A voice in John's ear said, 'I'm sorry, Mr Kermidge.'

It was Inspector Peddick.


Veronica worried about John for the next three weeks.
Although he was not ill, he showed no inclination to rise,
and began to grow a beard out of sheer indolence. He never
spoke except to say on one occasion, 'I'm a patriot, my
dear. I'm staying in bed to make it easy for the police. In
these hard days of intensive burglary and juvenile delin-
quency, it would be unfair to put too much pressure on the
Yard by moving around.'

Sir Humphrey came to the house once or twice, but John
just stared at the ceiling, refusing to say a word. Preparations were being made to launch John's rocket, and Sir

Humphrey, a kind of devoted man at heart, sought to cheer up Veronica by telling her that a peerage was in the air. 'Even if John bridles at being Lord Kermidge, he'd surely wish to see you Lady Kermidge.'

'I don't care so long as he eats.'

One night, some twenty-five days after John's attempt to fly to Zurich, the press the world over noticed mysterious and intensive diplomatic activity.

It was remarked by vigilant American journalists that the Secretary of State left a public dinner at Cincinnati in order to fly to Washington. A few minutes later, the President of the United States interrupted a fishing holiday and left for Washington by helicopter. The faces of these two dignitaries were exceptionally grave.

Newspapermen in Moscow observed that a meeting of the Supreme Soviet had been called at only an hour's notice and that grim-faced deputies were disrupting the traffic as they poured into the Kremlin. Areas were cordoned off, and the police were uncommunicative. In Paris, a crisis was stopped in midstream as a rumour spread, making the rising spiral of the cost of living seem frivolous indeed.

The Right Honourable Arthur Backworth left Chequers at four in the morning for Number 10 Downing Street. Observers caught a glimpse of his ashen face in the dark bowels of his Rolls-Royce.

The wires from America reported not only the unexpected presence of the President and the Secretary of State in the federal capital, but also of an unusual number of generals and admirals, all of them sullen and thunderous. Businessmen attempting transatlantic calls found that there were endless delays. Tempers were frayed the world over.

One of the last to know the reason why was John, who was fast asleep when Veronica and Bill burst into his room with all the morning papers. He glanced at the headline of the first paper and began to laugh, slowly at first, then hysterically, until the tears poured from his eyes in a stream, coursing through his young beard, staining his pyjama top. For a full quarter of an hour he laughed, weeping, moaning, gripping his sides, tearing the sheets with a delight which overlapped into anguish, panting like a dying man, and dragging Bill and Veronica with him in his lunatic joy. Suddenly the laughter stopped, and John, Bill, and Veronica looked at each other without energy, without emotion.

John, breathing deeply, took up the newspaper and read the headline again.

It said, in banner type, SWISS REACH THE MOON.

# A WORD IN THE WORLD'S EAR

Martha and Vitus Grobchek were married in 1915, and had hardly exchanged a word since 1916. They had no real friends, but their neighbours, who were now and then awakened in the night by her moaning and by his raucous voice dispensing sarcasm in Czech, wondered why they had ever stayed together.

Hiram Maltby, one neighbour, a parking attendant by profession, made the following statement to the police when the time came. 'He wasn't a guy who could get friendly with. You'd say "hi" or "good morning" or pass some remarks about the weather, and you'd get no reply. He acted just like you weren't there. We asked him into our place when they first moved in. He said O.K., but he never did come. We were never asked to visit with him. I figure he was angry, antisocial, I don't know the right word for it, but like I say, he wasn't a guy you could get friendly with.'

The neighbour in apartment 6G, on the other side, a Madame Zelda Lupcevic, had a slightly different story to tell. She was a dressmaker whose speciality was altering garments for people with inconsistent weights. She worked at home, and so had plenty of opportunity to hear all there was to hear through the thin walls. 'I pitied her,' she declared in her Balkan accent. 'Most time it was silence, just the noise of feet, or cooking. Then she talk, nice quiet. She was nice, quiet woman. She sometime talk half-hour and get no answer. Then, like from nowhere, his voice, angry, violent. Then perhaps plate fly, or break something, and then silence till next time. She was good woman, always smiling. I feel she like talk but afraid. He act like someone drink, but I never see him so he couldn't walk straight or

101

say bad word clear. I understand few word Czech, and I tell you, language very bad.'

At the time of their marriage, Martha was seventeen and Vitus twenty. In the first flush of womanhood, her consistent smiling was still very attractive, since she boasted a charming dimple on one cheek which evoked good humour in everyone who met her. Vitus was on the short side, but his natural sullenness gave him an earnestness which was impressive and which inspired the belief among his older relatives that he would go far. His father was a carpenter, but Vitus was evidently going to explore vaster horizons. The fact that he treated his parents somewhat abruptly was put down to his inner restlessness, to his impatience for success, and it was understood not only by the parents themselves but by the entire little Czech colony on 2nd Avenue and 75th Street.

Only gradually did it begin to dawn on everyone that here was no second Rockefeller in the making, but a man who enjoyed only the rewards of work, not the work itself. His wife's smile became braver, and as a consequence more irritating. In 1917, he left for the war, not because he had experienced a patriotic call, but because it meant a free trip away from home. Truth to tell, he rather enjoyed the war. Life was cheap to him, since it held so little. Apart from that, he liked the company of men. The camaraderie of the trenches afforded him the emotional comfort which he had never found with women. Swearing and drinking were for him a great liberation of the spirit, and rough talk about girls was infinitely more satisfying and less trouble than actual involvement with them. They were on the earth for man's convenience, to be slept with and to shut up.

Naturally, during the war, and after, for the brief period of occupation, he went with prostitutes, and only with prostitutes. He became very angry if they were of the sentimental type who sought to replace the absent sweetheart

in his mind and who tried to play out the time with sac-
charine banter. He was with them for a purpose, and was in
more of a hurry than the most callous of them. He would
even pay them extra not to open their mouths.

His was the only face in the Victory Parade which was
entirely unsmiling. He stared through the ticker tape like
a hypnotist, his light blue eyes expressionless. The care-free
days were over. The preparations for his home-coming were
touching. There was a cake, and Czech sausages, and liquor
which his parents could ill afford. Martha smiled, and wept,
and smiled, and smiled. Endless relatives kissed him. Four
days later he enlisted in the Merchant Marine.

He travelled the Indian Ocean and the China Sea, the
Baltic and the Caribbean, seeing nothing except the inside
of bars and brothels. He swore happily with his buddies,
fought them and others for the sheer pleasure of fighting,
and there were always cards instead of conversation. The
years passed, and he gloried in his immaturity, prided himself on his loneliness, and indulged to the full the kind of
emotional homosexuality which is the stamp of those who
have to prove their masculinity to each other every so often
by knocking each other cold and who gravitate towards
the armed services and other organizations where men can
be men without interference from women.

Life became a little gloomier with the outbreak of World
War II, since the harbours themselves were bereft of those
carefree comforts associated with them by tradition. Many
of them were blacked out, navigation became more hazard-
ous, and fights were interrupted by highly proficient, or-
ganized bodies of uniformed men who appeared from
nowhere in jeeps. All the time seemed to be spent loading or
unloading, or zigzagging cautiously in extreme climates
under the peremptory eye of the Navy. Everyone seemed
jittery, and even an incautiously lit cigarette was the

pretext for a punishment out of all proportion to the crime.

Vitus detested this war. It had brought in a new type of man, a man who somehow seemed to despise the old sweat in a friendly, inoffensive way, a man who admitted he was an amateur, but who was determined to master the mystery of the sea as quickly as he was able, so that he could be of use in the war effort and return to his chosen profession as soon as possible after victory. This manner of man brought the hated fragrance of home on to the high seas. He showed pictures of his wife and kids around, his face disfigured with paternal pride, and he clamoured for mail when it arrived like an animal at feeding time.

Some of these newcomers were of superior intelligence, and they quickly gained promotion. Vitus had never wanted promotion in the old days, since his anathema in this life was responsibility, but now that fellows who had invaded his tawdry empire less than a year ago were actually bossing him around, he became wildly jealous and morosely bitter by turns.

He spent quite a time in the cells, either on board or in various seaports, and in 1943, after a stormy interview with an overworked psychiatrist, he found himself back in New York with nowhere else to go but home. That week of unemployment was to him the longest week in his life. His wife suffered a severe shock when she saw him, but when she came to, there was that sickening, ever-ready smile again, so willing to forgive, so compliant, such an invitation for cruelty.

Martha had lived as best she could for the past twenty-eight years, working mostly as a waitress in a branch of a vast chain of cut-price caterers. She was known and liked by her colleagues not only because she was a willing worker but because she was so easy to forgive if she made a mistake. The smile which so maddened her husband was accepted by most people as an outward mark of inner sweetness.

Vitus was gratified that she was working, since it meant that he could take some money out of her bag and sit balefully in the bars on 3rd Avenue and wait for something to happen. It never did. There weren't even any really honourable fights. Here it was all pavements, and overcrowding, and patrolling policemen, all familiarity and dreariness, and no ship waiting with funnels smoking to carry him out of trouble if trouble came. After a week he got a job in a garage. He was given a pair of blue overalls with the words 'Klein's Friendly Garage Service' stitched back and front, and never can such winning sentiments have been more roundly contradicted by the face which crowned them. What really gave him the job was the fact that he volunteered for the night shift. This would mean that he saw his wife only on Sundays.

Martha had suffered greatly since her marriage. The gossip of the community, although aimed at her husband, could not fail to affect her. His parents had been very good to her, but their ready tears were hardly a consolation for her rancid hopes. She lived in patience, conquering her body's frantic desire for children with a peasant dignity. The local priest comforted her as best he could, by suggesting that God moves in mysterious ways, and she agreed, allowing herself to reflect that the ways of God were hardly as mysterious as those of her husband. The priest had understood her natural anguish, and she had been encouraged to take her mind off her personal tragedy by helping him in many ways.

Gradually she had come to be known as a saintly woman, and the local hatred for her husband grew. It was, however, during one of her visits to a hospital that her saintliness was put to its severest test. She met Jiri Smetacek, a young

invalid who knew he was destined to die and who had become calm and wise as dignity was thrust upon him prematurely. It was 1917. The emotional stability of all nations
was threatened. Husbands were away from home. The im-
permanence of existence was on every mind. The most unexpected desires gripped the most sedate people. This might
even be the end of the world, so why not sing, dance, make
love? The documents at the Last Judgment would be in
such confusion that they would take years to sort out.

What began as a platonic romance, a bringing of maga-
zines to the hospital every other day, suddenly blossomed
into something more dangerous when the doomed youth
began to recover rapidly against all the prognostications of
the doctors. His love for Martha seemed to have produced
a miracle, and by December of 1917 he was out of hospital.
The rest was only natural. The tidal wave of love which
Vitus had refused so coldly was unleashed on Jiri. They
spent hours in each other's arms, whispering of a future
which both knew could never be. Every gift of nature was
expended lavishly in those few months – laughter, tears,
silence, poetry, physical ecstasy, and sweet sleep. It proved
too much for Jiri. When spring came round again, Martha
was a woman, and he was dead.

She had known what it was to love, and therefore she
had known what it was to live. No one could ever take that
away from her, and her permanent smile had a pride about
it. When Vitus came back in 1919, she braced herself to
meet him, and although she wept, she fancied that she met
his eyes without appeal, on equal terms. It took her by surprise, however, when he left again so soon to join the Merchant Marine. Then, in her new solitude, she began to have
a doubt. Had anyone told him about Jiri? Did he know?
Was he really a decent man at heart; had the war cured
him of his disturbing sullenness; had he been ready to come

back to her again, and start afresh, when some gossip had told him about another man?

Nothing is less conducive to peace of mind than questions which have no chance of being answered. For twenty-five years she had gone to the cemetery once a week to put flowers on Jiri's grave, always choosing a time of day in which the place would be relatively empty, and loitering among the graves until she felt she was unobserved before she whispered the few words of love which kept her memory of him alive. Afterwards she would invariably surrender to a feeling of guilt about the man she knew so much less intimately than she had known her lover. The desire to forgive and be forgiven are an integral part of love; they are the rocks which humans use to trouble waters which have become stagnant by force of habit. And yet, here there was nobody to forgive, just an endless doubt, an endless pang of guilt, a memory of happiness, and solitude, which makes thoughts unhealthy.

It was natural for Martha to faint when Vitus came home without warning, after so many years in the Merchant Marine, but when he decided to go on night shift rather than enjoy the comfort of his wife, she began to wonder if that was his way of censuring her infidelity. She had nowhere to turn. The old priest had died. His place had been taken by a young man who could have been her son. One doesn't talk of such things to a stripling without experience of life.

Sundays seemed to last forever. She cooked, and Vitus ate. She washed up while he sat looking out of the window. Not a word passed between them. Eventually she bought a small television set out of her savings, just for the pleasure of hearing a human voice. He didn't seem to object. All he did occasionally was to change the programme.

\*    \*    \*

About this time, a man renowned for his goodness, a certain Professor Odin Strang Newville, acquired a television programme of his own. He had given syndicated advice to those in need of it for many years, and his beaming face was so well known to the nation that a couple of sponsors had deemed it worth their while to donate such a public service every Sunday on one of the channels. The programme had the slightly ambitious title of 'A Word in the World's Ear', and the idea behind it was to subject some personal problem to a committee of experts, who would give their advice freely. The person in need of help was shrouded in dramatic shadows on one side of the screen, while Professor Strang Newville himself, a certain Dr X, who was a psychiatrist, and a man named George Q. Nash, a public figure renowned for his sparkle, listened to the tale of woe and then debated the merits of the case before millions of listeners.

This programme was a very popular one in the Grobchek household, because Martha could derive some comfort from the misery of other people, while Vitus watched the proceedings with a look of icy hatred which strengthened his conviction that even if Heaven is up there, Hell is right here, and not a step down. Occasionally, he would mutter something like 'Serves her right' or 'I know what I'd do if I was that bitch's husband', which gave Martha the opportunity of hearing his voice.

Martha regarded Professor Strang Newville with the greatest reverence. Those round horn-rimmed glasses which often caught the studio lights gave him at those times an all-seeing quality, a radiance, which was amplified by the incessant murmur of the Hammond organ into something very close to divinity. His voice was so calm, so sure of itself, that it could only be transmitting the inflexible orders of another, still more beautiful voice, which only he could hear. Dr X was more tortured, more hesitant, with his face of a Saint Bernard forced to travel with its cask empty, but then he worked down among men, in the mud and grime of the secular spirit. George Q. Nash tried to look grave when the organ boomed its most inspirational chords, but something about him suggested that he knew he was being paid for his contribution and was, after much wrangling, satisfied with the fee.

It was the compelling presence of the professor, however, which drove Martha to commit the most reckless action of her life. She did as she was told at the end of the programme and wrote her application on a plain postcard to 'A Word in the World's Ear', being careful to give as an address her place of business. Having taken this step, she felt reborn. Around the clock she prepared what she should say, how she should present her case. In her dreams she was already on the programme and the professor touched Vitus with his magic wand, so that her husband was suddenly all smiles and forgiveness and whispering that it was not too late.

A week later she received an answer, which asked her to come for an interview. Taking time off from her work, she went to a penthouse on Madison Avenue, where she was disappointed not to see the professor himself but only a formal young lady wearing an explosion of rhinestones on her glasses, which appeared to be the only source of light in the cell-like room. As her eyes grew accustomed to the subdued lighting, Martha saw that the walls were covered with diplomas and awards which the professor had received for being a television personality, and his greatness seemed to her confirmed.

She answered the dispassionate questions of the interviewer as best she could. To her surprise, the interviewer gave no indication of being impressed, but just said, 'We'll let you know.'

'I'd be grateful,' said Martha, 'if there was no reference to my being Czech. It might make my husband suspicious.'

'O.K.,' answered the interviewer, 'we can settle all that with the professor when the time comes. Would Italian do?'

'Sure, anything but Czech.'

'I'll pencil in, Italian.'

Six weeks later, when Martha was beginning to feel rejected not only by her husband but also by society, a second letter arrived, telling her to appear at the studio on Sunday week. She began to make elaborate plans for explaining her absence to her husband, which were all quite useless since he evinced no interest in her activities whatsoever, and if she had announced that she was leaving forever, he would only have growled a request that she hand over her pay cheque for the week before going.

On the Tuesday before the show, she saw him for a few minutes before he left for the garage and announced that her Aunt Maria had asked her for tea on Sunday, and wasn't it nice of her. She had even called her aunt to tell her that if there were any inquiry by Vitus, they were having tea on Sunday. Aunt Maria was surprised, since she had not talked to Vitus since World War I and had no hope or intention of renewing the acquaintance, but agreed that she would be willing to supply an alibi if it were needed. Vitus, however, didn't react to the news of the imminent tea party.

When Sunday eventually came, Martha became desperately uneasy. She began to wonder if she had done the right thing. Her life was hateful, but it was calm. Her husband never spoke. He only cuffed her, or shouted at her when she was in his direct path and proved an obstacle to his progress across a room. A sudden thought of Jiri could dispel all pain. Now she was going to uproot all the memories, risk awakening emotions which had lain dormant, review the whole panorama of her disenchantment, in public, before millions of people. She kept looking at the clock in the kitchen. Often she thought it must be broken, since the minute hand moved so slowly. She made breakfast and washed up. She made lunch and washed up. Eventually, at half-past three, she summoned up all her courage and announced brightly that it was time to go. Vitus put his feet on the table and shut his eyes. She went.

There were two hours to kill before she had to report, so she walked. The weather was glorious, but she didn't notice it. She was busy pleading her case to an imaginary jury of wise and tolerant men. Strong arms came out to sustain her, noble faces mouthed words of comfort to her, the whole world understood her plight and cried out her heroism until the organ music in her head rocked the tears from her eyes and she saw only the sidewalk dancing before her. A taxi-driver cursed her. 'Make up your mind,' he shouted. She walked on, heedless of the traffic and of other people, until she reached the gigantic edifice in which she was to beat her breast and hear voices like Joan of Arc.

The professor was in the make-up room when she first saw him. There was a little hedge of tissues in his collar to prevent it from being soiled by the make-up, which was being cautiously applied by a man dressed as a surgeon. The professor's secretary sat by him as they planned the last details of the programme together.

'First is a Mrs Wilefski,' said the secretary.

'What's her problem?' asked the professor. 'Is she the one with the frigid husband?'

'No,' answered the secretary, 'she's the one who can't help herself from stealing.'

'Oh, yes. She's been in prison?'

'Yes.'

'And it's O.K. to mention that? Have we a written clearance from her?'

'Yes, we have.'

'Good. And then?'

'Then, Mrs Grobchek.'

Here Martha stepped forward and announced that she had been sent to be made up.

'There must be some mistake,' said the secretary, 'because we never see your face. We just hear your voice.'

'I'm glad,' said Martha.

The professor beamed. 'You are Mrs Wilefski,' he said, 'and we're going to do our level best to straighten out your problem. People who steal the kind of merchandise you've been stealing don't just do it to get rich quick. You do it because there's something inside you tells you to steal.'

'I'm Mrs Grobchek,' said Martha.

A little later, over coffee, the professor explained to her the format of the programme. 'You come on,' he said, 'just after the station break and the second commercial. That redhead over there, Betty, will beckon you in, and you will take your place in the armchair centre stage. This is so lit that you will be seen in silhouette only. Then you tell us a capsule story of your life in five minutes, after I have introduced you as Mrs B. We don't give away names on this show. Then both Dr X and Mr Nash will have the opportunity of asking you some questions, and I finally sum up our mutual impressions, and we send you on your way with our blessings. It's quite easy and quite painless. If you should feel yourself breaking down or upset, don't try to hold it back. This is a human interest programme, a show in which I try to reach people through people, that is my motto, reach people through people, so that we all may benefit from the experiences and the tragedies of those great enough in heart to share them with their fellows. And I want you to know how much I appreciate your visiting with us this afternoon.'

Soon afterwards the show began with a swirl of organ music. The professor faced his multitudinous flock and said, 'A Word in the World's Ear – and this is your moderator, Odin Strang Newville. Today we have two more cases with which to touch the conscience of society, two more words to whisper in the ear of a world too often callous, too often obsessed with its own everyday problems to heed the pleading of those rejected hearts which claim our attention from the fringes of life. But first, a word from our sponsor.'

Here everything stopped while two small animated gentlemen comically extolled the virtues of a deodorant on the screen. When they had finished, the wretched Mrs Wilefski was led to the fatal armchair and was introduced as Mrs A. She told the story of her kleptomania in a small, quivering voice. When she had finished, she was gently cross-examined by the panel and eventually dismissed by the professor with some ringing words of comfort.

Martha was about to step forward but was restrained, since the second half of the programme was presented by another sponsor, and the screen was temporarily occupied by a young lady in a bathing costume performing some embarrassingly carefree antics in a mountain pool, while a female chorus chanted a jingle about mint in a cooler-than-just-cool cigarette. At last the commercial was over, and the redheaded girl led Martha to her place of execution.

She was terribly nervous, but when the professor smiled at her and said, 'Good evening, Mrs B,' there was such warmth and compassion in his voice that she felt strong again. 'Mrs B, you are Italian,' said the professor.

'Yes.'

'Will you now tell the panel what brought you here?'

With rising emotion, Martha told her story, and when it was indicated to her by an impatience in the gestures of the professor that her five minutes were up, she didn't feel she had managed to tell the half of it.

'Let me get this clear,' said George Q. Nash. 'You married in 1915, and you noticed almost immediately that your husband's love for you, his attentions, shall we say, were abnormal in that they were non-existent.'

'Yes.'

'In 1917, he volunteered to go to war, and four days after his return he entered the Merchant Service, and you didn't see him again until 1943?'

'Yes.'

'Did he write?'

'No.'

'Never?'

'Never.'

'And the word "divorce" was never mentioned by either party, either before 1917 or after 1943?'

'No.'

'Are you very religious people?'

'I don't think he is. I used to be.'

'You used to be – until your love affair with the other man?'

'Yes.'

'But why did you think that your lapse would debar you from the comfort of religion? Surely the fact that you had sinned would be calculated to make you even more needful of that comfort which only religion can bring to those who are blessed with belief?'

'I didn't think I was worthy of the Church – and in any case my husband hates the Church. I don't know if he hates the Church really, but he hates priests.'

'Don't you think that a visit to a priest would help as far as you are concerned?'

'Not really, no. No longer.'

George Q. Nash shook his head gravely. He disliked

priests too, and hadn't been to church since his confirmation, but he was a public figure, with a public following.

Dr X asked a few questions. 'Tell me, do you have a sneaking suspicion that your husband knows about your affair with the other man?'

'I don't know. Sometimes I do, at other times I don't.'

'Do you occasionally wonder if it isn't some small detail which has poisoned your relationship? Don't you sometimes try to pin it down to one single event or fact?'

'Yes.'

'You say he is an uncommunicative man. Well, sometimes men are uncommunicative because they are at base shy, even timid. This could also account for his abruptness, his sudden changes of mood. Men who vacillate, and who know they vacillate, will often try to hide their weakness by overdoing the illusion of strength which they wish to create. He may well have known all about your infidelity but be too basically timid to bring the subject up, and his own irritation with himself leads him into this sullenness you speak about.'

'Yes, that's possible,' said Martha, although she hardly recognized this as a portrait of her husband.

'You see,' said Dr X, 'everything you say about him points to a certain immaturity. You say he was always somewhat sulky in manner, but when you married he was still very young and unsure of himself. It could be – I'm not saying that it is – it could be that his discovery of your infidelity flung him back into that mood in which he found the greatest security and which prevented him from ever really growing up.'

'If this is so, what can I do?' asked Martha, horrorstruck.

'This affair of yours took place in 1917. Surely by now there is only one thing to do. Tell him about it. That is perhaps what he is most longing to hear. He can't bring himself to accuse you of it, especially now that so much time has passed. It would sound almost ridiculous. But if you did it, it might well, even at this late stage, bring out all the love and affection which are at the moment bottled up inside him. There must have been a reason for you two to have married in the first place. Since then, those emotions have been forcibly hibernating. Make a clean breast of it, tell him, honestly and fearlessly, of your lapse, and if he is half a man, it's my guess he will forgive you there and then, and you will both have a chance of happiness which is the birthright of us all.'

'I quite agree,' said George Q. Nash. 'If he has a vestige of a sense of humour, you will be laughing about all this tomorrow. It's a very sad story, but it also has its amusing side, or would have if it were a work of fiction instead of fact. Nearly forty years of silence occasioned by one misunderstanding! Of course you must tell him. After all, things are bad enough, Mrs B. Ask yourself, what have you to lose?'

As the organ broke into an ethereal coda, Professor Strang Newville added his own wisdom to the verdict. 'Yes, go home, your head held high, Mrs B., and find it in yourself to look your husband in the eye and to tell him that you are human, and being human, you have sinned. Ask his forgiveness, with humility but not without dignity, for he too has sinned in his treatment of you. Do this simple thing, and you will find an old age replete with the comfort which youth and maturity have denied you. It is never too late to start living.'

Martha rode home in a bus, her head awhirl with so much psychology. Things were never what they seemed in this modern, complicated civilization into which she had survived. Wonderful what man had invented for his use, and sad that she could only obey without understanding.

When she reached her apartment block, she was suddenly obsessed with a fear that Vitus might have watched the show. Her accent wasn't Italian, whatever the professor might have said. And her voice might have given her away. The pundits had made a great point of the fact that her story was unusual. If Vitus had been listening, he could hardly have failed to recognize it. It was not until just after nine o'clock that she entered the apartment, white and haggard, to find Vitus in a flaming temper. He shouted, roared, and smashed some plates, then sent her flying across the room into a chest of drawers.

Trembling, she asked him, 'Did you see the show?'

'What show?' he cried. 'Think I've got nothing better to do than watch TV when you're not around? I've been out, and I came back at eight for dinner. What are you trying to do, starve me or something?'

The neighbours started hammering on the wall, and Vitus hammered back like a madman while she was cooking. The moment was not propitious for a confession of infidelity.


All that week she tried to summon up courage, but there was hardly the opportunity. She was forced to wait until the next Sunday, when perhaps the glowing face of the professor would inspire her once again to look deep into her soul and find the necessary strength there. And so it happened that late the next Sunday afternoon, she switched on her television set. Vitus was reading a science-fiction comic he had bought at a back-date magazine emporium, and he seemed to raise no objection to the television. When the set warmed into life, the kindly face of the professor appeared.

'A Word in the World's Ear,' he said, 'and this is your moderator, Odin Strang Newville. Today we have two more cases with which to touch the conscience of society, two more words to whisper in the ear of a world too often callous—'

Suddenly the urgency of this brilliant man's message came alive to Martha. She remembered every word of the panel's advice to her as though it had just been told her. 'He will forgive you there and then, and you will both have a chance of happiness which is the birthright of us all.' 'You will be laughing about all this tomorrow.' 'Find it in yourself to look your husband in the eye and to tell him that you are human, and being human, you have sinned.'

'Vitus,' she said, in a loud, clear voice.

'Shut up.'

'Vitus, there is something I must tell you.'

'Can't you see I'm reading?' But he looked up in spite of himself, so surprising was her tone of voice.

'I am only human,' she declared.

'So what, who isn't?'

'I am only human, and being human, I have sinned.'

'What's the matter with you? Got religion or something?'

'I want to tell you what I think you already know, only I want to tell it to you in my way.'

She was speaking with great difficulty and tremendous intensity, and he couldn't find words with which to interrupt her.

'I haven't always been a good wife to you.'

Now he could relax. 'Who cares?' he said.

'You remember Jiri Smetacek?'

'No. Now shut up.'

'I slept with him. I gave myself to him.'

Vitus looked at her and laughed, almost merrily.

She could scarcely believe her eyes. His face seemed human. The wise men had been right.

'When?' asked Vitus.

'In 1917.'

'When I was away . . . at the war?'

His face clouded with rage, and his blue eyes protruded. Viciously he pushed a chair away with his foot, then grew calm as ice and left the room.

'Where are you going?' cried Martha, petrified.

He came back with a kitchen knife and killed her with a single blow. Her scream echoed through the still Sunday, and the neighbours phoned for the police of their own accord, without consulting each other or bothering to inquire what had been going on.

Vitus was reading his comic book when the police arrived, and he seemed surprised to see them. He was quite calm and friendly and told them for their benefit as they examined Martha's corpse, 'If I'd been younger, I'd have fought the lot of you, and won. I ain't afraid of you. I ain't afraid of no man.'

The only trace of bitterness in him came at one moment when, out of the blue, he said, 'Women, can't trust 'em,' and spat on the floor.

In the drama of the moment, no one had thought of turning off the television set, and so it was that, as they led Vitus away and covered Martha with a sheet, the professor's reassuring face was still visible on the screen, and he was saying, 'If you wish to put your case before the panel, write to me, Odin Strang Newville, A Word in the World's Ear, Box 75157, New York, and remember, write your problem on a plain postcard. I will repeat the address . . .'

# THERE ARE 43,200 SECONDS IN A DAY

Edwin Applecote used to go to the zoo, not to see the lions, but to see the rabbits. Nature he considered marvellous, because every facet of man, every temperament, was reflected in it. The comptroller of his department at the British Broadcasting Corporation was a lion by nature, a red-bearded Scot with a slow but diabolical temper, forever wrapped in hairy tweeds. Miss Butler, the producer of his programme, was a bit of a horse, even more of a gnu, that South African animal with a vast, horny nose and tiny hangover eyes. Mustn't be cruel to Miss Butler, though. She might not be a thing of beauty, but she had a beautiful spirit. Miss Mowberry, who ran the section devoted to music and movement for the under-fours, was a hen. When she performed her callisthenics on a toe she imagined to be both light and fantastic, she bore a terrible resemblance to a hen rushing in panic from under the wheels of an approaching car. Miss Alsop, the lyric soprano, was a giraffe. Her neck was so long that you could practically follow the notes on the way from the diaphragm into the open air. And he, Edwin Applecote, the high tenor, was a rabbit.

His mother had been an old maid by inclination, and his father a confirmed bachelor. They had married late in life, and it had been a union of two habitual wallflowers. Edwin always blushed at the thought of the process which had given him life, since his parents had always seemed to him far too nice to forget themselves in such an intensely personal way. It only happened once, however. He was an only child.

He had been very close to his mother, but then he had been very close to his father also, since his parents had resembled each other in the most remarkable way, and there was nothing left for him but to resemble them both. Family life had been harmonious, with never an angry word exchanged. Breakfast had been taken at 8.00, lunch at 1.00 sharp, tea at 4.30, supper at 7.45. Mr Applecote had worked as an assistant in a draper's shop all his life with no thought of promotion. Although a devout man, neither God nor even the King were the figures who crowned his imagination, but Mr Perry, the owner of the shop he worked in. Mr Perry this, and Mr Perry that, dominated every conversation, and Mrs Applecote was tactful enough to ask, 'What did Mr Perry say today?' when she caught her husband daydreaming for a moment.

Even in death his parents had been decent and undramatic, each dying during sleep, the expressions on their faces untroubled by pain, doubt, or even experience.

Edwin had had an average education, and had culled average marks. He hated games, but was too timid to admit it, and so threw himself into them with touching abandon, his games master describing him as a 'tryer'. The Army discharged him after six months for anaemia, and he had found a job near the end of the war, while the competition was negligible, which both suited his temperament and enabled him to eat.

For sixteen years now he had worked on the children's radio programme, singing nursery rhymes with Miss Alsop, and lending his voice to an animated puppet called Siegfried, who was a top-hatted rabbit, and a great favourite with the kids.

This work gave him considerable free time, and there was nothing he liked better than to spend his hours of leisure at the zoo, watching the small defenceless creatures of nature engaged in their harmless pursuits. He knew a way of reaching the houses in which they were kept without going too near the large and dangerous mammals.

Whenever he was compelled to pass the lions and the tigers, he would imagine ways in which he could save himself if by some chance one of them escaped while he was in the vicinity. He eyed every railing, judging its height, and would walk a little quicker when he was nowhere near a door.

In traffic, too, he would sometimes remain alone on the pavement while a herd of people crossed against the light, trusting in safety in numbers. He could not mount or dismount from a moving bus, nor could he face the escalator in the subway. He was haunted by visions of catching his foot in the machine, and often dreamed about it. The electric rail both fascinated and terrified him, and he couldn't bring himself to travel that way during the rush hour, for fear of being pushed on to it by the crowd. Elevators were another conveyance of which he had a mortal fear. If the car suddenly should drop, he often wondered if it wouldn't be possible to jump in the air at the moment of impact with the bottom, and made elaborate plans for just such a contingency.

Once he had tried to ride a bicycle, and had found it fairly easy to retain his balance, but the sound of any internal combustion engine behind him made him wobble and eventually fall. Being a very phlegmatic person, basically, he needed no psychiatric assistance, since no wise man would ever make him braver, and it was merely association with other people, with crowds and machines and open spaces which confused him. Alone, at home, with his few bits of Victorian furniture, his brown velvet curtains, and his odds and ends, all inherited and remembered with affection from the days of a poor but untroubled youth, he felt entirely confident and controlled.

When he made himself some tea, and it was often, he laid all the dainty implements out as though he were expecting company. He sipped the tea out of a cup decorated with fading roses, and passed a few polite remarks about it in a small, high voice, taking nine or ten minute mouthfuls to dispose of a scone, and wiping his hands on a mono-grammed napkin as though trying to remove bloodstains afterwards. He always washed up after every meal, wearing a mauve apron which had been his mother's. The place was invariably spotless, even if it smelled of age, dampness, and the acrid odour of metholated spirit used to clean the pewter mugs and horse brasses which hung, cottage-like, around the mantelpiece.

This peaceful haven was a two-room apartment on the second floor of a low house in Bayswater, London, north of the park. It is an area of decaying opulence, which finally received its *coup de grâce* during the war, when the bombs felled buildings which would have fallen down anyway. The only other occupant of the house was a Mrs Sidney, whom Edwin often greeted in the entrance hall, since she appeared to go in and out of her flat with extraordinary frequency. She was a polite lady with a careworn expres-sion and a common voice, and her perfume was disagree-ably intense. A Sealyham terrier?

One summer's day Edwin finished his radio programme a little earlier than usual, and after returning home briefly for tea, he sped to the zoo in a bus. He pursued his usual complicated path to his friends, the rabbits. He stayed there a full two hours, reflecting that there is no greater consola-tion in life than to find a creature who shares your fears. So long as rabbits were part of nature, with their innocent eyes and contented chewing, he was just a timid man, not a freak.

When he emerged into the open, it was already begin-ning to get dark. The zoo was on the point of closing for the night, and he hurried back the way he had come, only to find about halfway to the turnstile that his path was blocked by a barrier. They had begun to work on some underground cables. There was nothing for it, he had to retrace his steps and take the shorter road by the lion house. He began to run, not only because of his fear of being locked in the zoo for the night, but also because the lions were in a fretful mood, and roaring.

The twilight played all manner of cruel tricks on him. As he ran, he believed he saw shapes moving before him, crouching in the shadows, encircling him silently. He staggered through the turnstile and stood for five minutes in the street, leaning on a lamp-post, recovering his breath. His thin white brow was beaded with perspiration. It was a bad way to start an evening.

The bus stopped near his home, and he was about to step off, when, with a lurch, it left again. He remonstrated with the conductor, who was not very helpful, but at least made sure that he got off at the next stop before it left again. As he alighted, he apologized to the conductor out of force of habit, although he had absolutely nothing to apologize about.

He walked back towards his home absently, his imagination crowding with leaping lions and crouching pumas. Oh dear, if it was like this when he was awake, what would it be like when he was asleep? He would have to take a pill and set the alarm. Near his front door, he looked up and saw the police. Not one bobby, but four of them, a squad car, an ambulance, and a couple of plainclothes men.

He stopped dead. This was worse than lions. He couldn't see their eyes, which were hidden in the shadow of their hats and helmets, but there was no mistaking the fact that they were looking at him. What had he done? His radio licence had been posted on time, unless it had been mislaid in the mail. The rent had been paid, and the rates. His income tax was deducted at source. During the war, his record had been impeccable as far as his rations were concerned. Admittedly, he had accepted a little extra sugar, but only from a diabetic friend. He had a sweet tooth. Was that a crime? And if it was, did it warrant an entire platoon of policemen and detectives?

The longer he stood there, the more guilt he felt. Suddenly, he could stand the tension no longer. He turned and walked away. Behind him he could hear one, two, three footfalls. This was like riding a bicycle. The feet seemed to be gaining on him. He walked faster. As he passed a lamp-post, he saw his shadow lengthen grotesquely, and just before he walked out of range of the light, the shadows of three helmets shot past his feet like arrows and disappeared into the gloom. At the next lamp-post, the three helmets were closer behind him. He started to run and reached the road. Here he paused in order to be certain that no traffic was approaching. He looked right, left, right again, as he had been taught in the propaganda against jay-walking, and they caught him.

'Are you Edwin Applecote?' asked a stout policeman.

'No.'

'You aren't Edwin Applecote?'

'Yes,' said Edwin, crestfallen.

'Then why did you say you wasn't?'

'I don't know, sir. I lost my head.'

'What made you run away?'

'Same reason, I suppose. What have I done?'

'I don't know. We want you to answer a few questions.'

'What about?'

'There's been a murder.'

'Murder?'

Edwin fainted in the arms of the policeman who was standing behind him, and they carried him back to his house.

Detective-Inspector McGlashan saw the strange cortège approaching and called out, 'Did you get him?'

He was a no-nonsense man with a glorious record in the

Western Desert, where Montgomery had helped him to win the campaign.

His eyes narrowed as he said, 'Resisted, did he? The blighter.'

'No, fainted,' answered Constable Matley. 'Fainted clear away when he heard there'd been a murder.'

They put Edwin in the gutter to rest.

'So that's Applecote, is it?' snarled McGlashan. 'Pretty poor specimen.'

'I'd say he weighed about ninety pounds,' laughed Matley. 'Some people have all the luck.'

Constable Norton was very young. Seeing the intense expression on McGlashan's face, he said, excitedly, 'You don't think he did it, do you, sir?'

McGlashan shot a withering look at the boy.

'I know, Norton, that in the detective stories, criminals always return to the scene of their crime, but they usually allow a decent interval of time to elapse. If you committed a murder, would you come back an hour later?'

'No, sir.'

'Why not?'

'Well . . . well . . .'

'You'd be frightened that you'd run headlong into the police, wouldn't you?'

'Yes, sir.'

'Very well, then, stop talking through the back of your head.'

'Yes, sir.' Norton wasn't defeated. His keen young face lit up again.

'Of course, he may be a loony, sir.'

McGlashan looked sourly at Edwin.

'I wouldn't put it past him at that,' he growled.

'Where am I?' asked Edwin, who was in time to see a body being carried from his house on a stretcher.

'Hold it,' said McGlashan to the stretcher-bearers, and then turning to Edwin, asked, 'Did you know Mrs Sidney?'

'Yes – that is, I didn't know her exactly.'

'You'd recognize her if you saw her again?'

'Oh, yes. She's been living here for over three years.'

McGlashan helped Edwin to his feet and walked him to the stretcher.

With a brisk, unemotional gesture, he pulled the blanket away to reveal the face of Mrs Sidney, hideously mangled and spattered with blood.

Edwin screamed and fainted again. McGlashan caught him and called in a disgusted voice, 'It's her all right. Norton, Mayhew, get him off me.'

The pathologist, Dr Golly, came slowly out of the house.

'She's been dead less than an hour,' he said. 'Evidently she didn't die at once.'

'Of course not. She called the police,' said McGlashan.

'Death was caused by the cumulative effects of a beating, both with fists and with a stick, as far as I can see at the moment. She had been drinking. Very sordid.'

Edwin was white. He had a splitting headache, and wished to be sick.

'Let's go up to your flat,' said McGlashan.

'All right.'

Edwin led the way, but stopped when he saw some dark patches on the wooden floor of the entrance hall.

'What's that?' he asked.

'Blood.'

Edwin vomited, and then declared that he couldn't stay there a moment longer.

They took him to the station and gave him a cup of tea. As he drank it, he was composed enough to reflect that their tea wasn't a patch on his.

'Now,' said McGlashan, 'where were you an hour ago, that is about seven-fifteen to seven-thirty?'

'I was at the zoo.'

'The zoo closes at six.'

'Not in summer.'

McGlashan nodded. Edwin had escaped from that trap.

'What were you doing at the zoo?'

'I often go.'

'That's no answer.'

'I like the zoo. I go to look at the animals.'

'Which animals?'

'Lions, tigers, all animals,' he lied, and blushed. He was seized with a feeling that he had deserted his little friends. 'Rabbits,' he added lamely.

'Rabbits,' said McGlashan, with more intensity than the word could carry. He lit a cigarette in order to appear casual.

'Cigarette?'

'I never smoke nor drink. May I have a butterscotch pastille? They steady me.'

McGlashan was beginning to wonder whether Edwin wasn't slightly mad, or perhaps just acting stupid.

'You say you go to the zoo often. You must have a very special kind of work to get so much free time.'

'I work for the B.B.C.'

'What are you, a sports commentator?'

'Oh, lordie, no. I work on the new children's programme *Come out to Play*, at three-fifteen daily.'

'My daughters watch that.'

'Do they!' cried Edwin with delight. 'How old are they?'

'One's five, one's two.'

'Ah, the two-year-old would be a little young to understand.'

'She's old for her age.'

'Has she any favourites?'

'Wumbly the Mule.'

'Ah, yes, that's Miss Alsop.'

'I beg your pardon?'

'Miss Alsop lends her voice to Wumbly. I do Siegfried the Rabbit.'

'Rabbit,' said McGlashan, putting two and two together and finding no satisfaction in the result. 'Give me your autograph, will you, for Jennifer?'

'Really? D'you mean it?' Edwin hesitated. 'But this is an official document.'

'Doesn't matter.' McGlashan smiled wanly. 'It's O.K. I'm not tricking you into confessing to a crime you didn't commit. Just sign Siegfried the Rabbit if you wish.'

Edwin did so, feeling that there was warmth in the coldest heart if you probed long enough.

'Now,' said McGlashan, pocketing the autograph, 'let's get down to cases. You often saw Mrs Sidney?'

'Oh, poor lady, yes, indeed I did. She always seemed to be going in or out.'

McGlashan smiled grimly.

'I'm not surprised, seeing the nature of her work, are you?'

'What exactly was the nature of her work, sir? I often wondered, but I didn't wish to appear inquisitive. I always imagined she must have had private means.'

McGlashan stared at him, incredulous.

'How long have you been living there?' he asked.

'Three years.'

'And how long has Mrs Sidney been living there?'

'She was there when I moved in.'

'You noticed nothing?'

'I noticed that she seemed very popular. She was always receiving visitors. In fact, truth to tell, I was a little puzzled that she never asked me in. After all, I was her neighbour.' He smiled sadly. 'She used to play her radio at all hours, but I didn't really mind. I never liked to bother her. Every

A.D.O.P.—7

time I went down to ask her up for a cup of tea, I could hear through the door that she had company.'

There was a pause.

'Don't sit on the edge of the chair,' said McGlashan. 'Lean back. We don't want you to faint again.' He cleared his throat. 'Mrs Sidney was a common harlot.'

'A what?' asked Edwin politely.

'A strumpet, a tart.'

'I'm sorry, I don't understand.'

McGlashan rolled his eyes with exasperation and brought his fist down on his desk. Steadied, he put on a sweet expression and said, 'A lady of easy virtue.'

'Oh no,' whispered Edwin, turning purple. 'Mrs Sidney? Surely not.'

'She picked up customers in the park and brought them back to the flat below yours.'

For the first time in his life, Edwin lost his temper. 'How disgusting!' he cried in his small voice.

His display of spirit had taken a lot out of him, and he was obviously in no condition to continue answering questions. As he only had very little money on him and clearly couldn't face his own apartment, McGlashan lent him a pound, and the police found him a room in a small hotel in the area. After he had gone, Constable Matley asked McGlashan whether any information had been gleaned from Edwin.

'No,' McGlashan grunted. 'He's a dear little fellow, but he's going to be a bloody awful witness when the time comes,' and then added, 'I don't know how a man like that can survive in this day and age.'

Edwin didn't sleep a wink all night, and he worried his colleagues at work. He forgot the words of *Oranges and Lemons* right in the middle of the programme, and seemed quite unable to take a prompt from Miss Alsop. Siegfried the Rabbit was particularly morose that day, and even incoherent. Mothers all over England telephoned to complain that their children had been unable to understand all that Siegfried had said.

He cashed a cheque and bought a shirt, but couldn't bring himself to go anywhere near the zoo. He returned to the hotel, and just sat down, staring at nothing. At half-past six, McGlashan dropped round. 'Cheer up,' he said.

Edwin hardly reacted.

McGlashan sat down on the bed.

'The main thing is to take an interest in what's going on,' he said. 'Don't let your mind go blank. You'll have a breakdown.'

'Take an interest in what?'

'In our work. You're part of the case, you know. Seen the evening paper?'

'No.'

McGlashan put it on Edwin's lap.

The headlines announced that a man had been arrested for the murder of Gertrude O'Toole, otherwise Mrs Sidney.

'Yes,' said McGlashan, 'we got him this morning. An easy case. I'm glad we got him that quick. The public was beginning to get restless. So many unsolved murders. We found some letters from him in her handbag, and we picked him up early this morning, asleep on a bench on the Embankment.'

'Who is he?' asked Edwin involuntarily.

'A pimp.'

'A what?'

The devil wouldn't know where to begin tempting this one. McGlashan felt he was dealing with a clergyman's daughter.

'A man who lives on the immoral earnings of a woman or women,' said McGlashan, making it sound as natural as he could.

'How is that possible?' asked Edwin, his voice trembling.

'The woman earns the money by soliciting, then she gives most of it to her male friend. Women who live that way are curious emotionally. They only live half a life, and this crazy kind of generosity may be their gesture towards the normal life they're forced to do without. I don't know. I'm not a psychologist. I just see the seamy side of life, recognize its patterns, but beyond that I'm not qualified to go. Can't change anything.'

'But what about the men . . . the men who accept such money?'

Edwin's face was a mask of real suffering, of horror.

McGlashan kept the tone of his voice as relaxed as he was able, almost weary.

'There'll always be men who think it's smart to get something for nothing, just as there'll always be men who think the male sex is superior to the female. Their instincts invariably seem to lead them to women who agree with them, and who get a vicious kick out of being victimized and pushed around.' McGlashan was an intelligent, even an interesting man. His undoubted physical courage was matched by an inquiring and often paradoxical mind which hardly seemed to suit his very active face. He recognized that it took all sorts to make a world, and he was not content with just saying so as a platitude when the occasion arose.

Now he sat facing Edwin, dealing with the situation with the tenderness of a regular sergeant who realizes that some wretched conscript is totally unsuited to his life, and that he is doing his unit more harm than good by his presence there. He leaned forward confidentially.

'I know all these facts are pretty shocking to you, Applecote, but these things exist, and we're not being quite realistic if we try to pretend they don't. Mind you, I'm not telling you all this just in order to get a rise out of you, or to see you flinch. I realize you must have lived a pretty sheltered life, or you'd hardly be surprised by all this. You'd have known Mrs Sidney for what she was. You might even have moved house. But look here, you're bound to be called on to give evidence—'

'Me?' cried Edwin.

'Yes.'

'I'd die!'

'No, you won't die. I just don't want you to make a fool of yourself when the time comes. I don't want you to stand up there and pretend you didn't know what Mrs Sidney was up to. Nobody'd ever believe you.'

'You believe me, don't you?' asked Edwin, averting his eyes.

'I believe you, but it took me nearly twenty-four hours, and you won't be that long in the witness-box. Some of these legal guys are tough customers. Too tough, I think. None of them care much for the police, that's how I know. If it should be Sir Cleverdon Bowyer or Sir Giles Parrish prosecuting, well, they're pretty impatient and sarcastic. They're out to rattle you. They want a conviction more than they want the truth.'

'Oh, I don't believe that, not in England.'

'Anywhere, Applecote. They're like boxers. They've got their reputations to think of, same as you and I. And the way they lose their reputations is by losing cases.'

Edwin became sullen and uncommunicative, so McGlashan rose and went to the door.

'I'm going to be proud of you,' he said.

'I owe you a pound,' said Edwin.

'Never mind about that now—' For the first time McGlashan was embarrassed, and he left.

Back at the station, he confided in Constable Matley.

'I don't give a damn for the killer, he's got it coming to him. I'm worried about Applecote, though. If he falls foul of Bowyer or Parrish, they'll eat him up. Silly to call him really, but I bet they do.'

After a few days the producer of Edwin's show, Miss Butler, took him aside and asked him if he was ill. He obviously couldn't concentrate properly, his complexion was appalling, there were pendulous bags under his eyes, and everyone in the department was very concerned about him. He blurted out the truth to her and burst into tears. They were all very kind and understanding, and he was given a week's leave with pay to recuperate.

This enforced absence did him no good whatsoever, since he just sat in his hotel and brooded for four days, eating nothing and sleeping not at all. On the fifth day, he was summoned as a witness for the prosecution. He was expecting this, since he had been interviewed by the clerk of the redoubtable Sir Cleverdon Bowyer, who was prosecuting in the trial of Arnold Ahoe, the alleged murderer. The meeting had passed in a dream, and Edwin could remember nothing of it. He was invaded by a great feeling of emptiness. He could no longer see clearly. Black, livery spots exploded in his eyes, and strange embryonic shapes kept passing sideways across his vision. There was a high, distant song in his ears.

He sat waiting to be called without emotion. Then at last he heard his name chanted by what sounded like an army of toastmasters, and he emerged into the courtroom. The glands at the back of his neck were swollen, and the nerves contorted. Every time he moved his head, it was as though a cargo of packing-cases were shifting from one temple to the other in a rough sea.

The judge, Lord Stobury, had the characteristic traits of his profession. A vulture's head was set below the hunched line of the shoulders, the white wig seeming to be powdered with the dust of death. It was hard to tell whether the eyes were open or shut, since the shadows which the brow cast on the eyelids looked strangely like dull, dark pupils. Behind Lord Stobury, a vast lion and unicorn propped up the arms of the realm on the wall, their expressions vindictive and intolerant. Sir Cleverdon Bowyer stood with his thumbs in his waistcoat pocket, a picture of assured arrogance, his single uninterrupted black eyebrow hanging like a canopy over his steel-grey eyes. Mr Herbert Ammons, the council for the defence, sat with the florid benignity of a fresh Dutch cheese on a welcoming buffet, expressing nothing as yet, his lips curved maliciously in repose. Ahoe, the prisoner, stood listlessly in the dock, an insignificant enough man who seemed quite unworthy of being the pretext for this heraldic assemblage.

This, then, was the place where British justice was dispensed, the place where men were told that they were innocent until proved guilty, but where the atmosphere told them that they were pretty guilty even if proved innocent. Edwin took the oath, and Sir Cleverdon wheeled himself into the position of assault like a wicked piece of artillery. He was a man who had done everything in his life with skill and application. In the 1930s he had run a mile in only very little over four minutes, he had represented his country in a bobsleigh on the Cresta Run, he had won races as a yachtsman and a rally driver, and he had once taken ten games off Tilden. Now he looked as though he were embarking on a sporting contest which he intended to win.

'You are Edwin Applecote?'

'Yes,' said Edwin inaudibly.

'Do I pronounce your name right? Is it Cote or Cott?'

'Whichever you prefer.'

'You are really most accommodating. You live, as I understand it, in the flat above that of Mrs Sidney, the murdered woman?'

'Yes.'

'How long have you lived there?'

'Three years.'

The judge interrupted.

'You must speak up,' he said. 'I can't hear the answers, and I must hear the answers. That is the cardinal rule of giving evidence. Whatever you say, be audible at all times.'

Edwin bowed elaborately.

'Proceed.'

The questions at the beginning were fairly pedestrian, since Sir Cleverdon was sure of victory.

'You were, of course, aware of the fact that she was a common harlot,' he said suddenly, after several minutes.

'No,' said Edwin, his eyes shut. This was terrible, terrible, all these questions in public.

Sir Cleverdon looked up, quick as lightning.

'You were not aware of the fact that the woman was a harlot? Come, come, do you expect me to believe that?'

He shot a look at his clerk, who was completely dumbfounded. In the preliminary meeting, Edwin had said everything McGlashan had told him to say, but now, for some reason, he was being utterly honest.

'Is it not a fact,' Sir Cleverdon proceeded, 'that the deceased was in the habit of entertaining frequently?'

'Yes.'

'She arranged her entertainments so that there was only one guest at a time, did she not?'

'I don't know.'

'Well, you never saw any women entering her apartment, did you?'

'Not that I can recall, sir.'

'Did you see men enter her apartment?'

'On one or two occasions, yes.'

'Did you ever see the prisoner enter Mrs Sidney's apartment?'

Edwin looked at Arnold Ahoe.

'I can't tell without my glasses, sir.'

'Have you got them with you?'

'Yes.'

'Then put them on by all means,' Sir Cleverdon thundered, his face suffused with irritation. 'Well?'

'I may have done. I can't be sure.'

'You can't be sure?' Sir Cleverdon repeated incredulously.

'Yes, I think I have seen the gentleman before, but I wouldn't know where I'd seen him.'

'The gentleman?'

There was a ripple of laughter in court. Even the prisoner grinned bleakly. The judge rapped his gavel.

Sir Cleverdon had never come across anything like it. What Edwin had said before was entirely different, and Sir Cleverdon was relying upon him to establish an odious and salacious character for the deceased, and therefore, by implication, for the company she kept.

'Do you feel quite well?' asked Sir Cleverdon.

'I haven't been feeling very well recently.'

'Perhaps in that case it would be better if we were to excuse you from testifying until such a time as you feel better.'

Mr Ammons was on his feet at once, his cheeks flushed with the pressure of blood and ambition.

'If my honourable and learned friend has finished his cross-examination, I would like to ask the witness a few questions.'

'The witness is ill, m'lud,' Sir Cleverdon remonstrated.

'He seems able to stand,' said the judge in chilly tones, 'he is vertical and breathing. The idea that he is ill emanated from you.' The judge looked over his glasses at Edwin. 'Would you describe yourself as ill?'

Edwin felt a great temptation to give up, but he was too truthful.

'No, my lord.'

'Very well. Have you finished your cross-examination, Sir Cleverdon?'

'For the time being, m'lud,' said Sir Cleverdon bitterly.

'Proceed, Mr Ammons.'

This is what Sir Cleverdon most feared. He leaned back and whispered furiously to his clerk, who shrugged his shoulders and wrung his hands.

A pinched smile spread over Ammons's face, a smile of conditional friendship.

'Mr Applecote, what is the nature of your employment?'

'I'm employed by the B.B.C., sir.'

'The British Broadcasting Corporation,' said Ammons, turning towards the jury, and making it sound like a piece of the national heritage. 'What function do you serve in that august body?'

'I work on the programme for children, *Come Out to Play*.'

'As an artist?'

'As a singer, sir.'

'And how long have you been employed in such a manner?'

'About sixteen years, sir.'

'Sixteen years!' cried Ammons, as though it were a century. He grasped his lapels and lowered his head for the charge. 'In other words, the British Broadcasting Corporation has seen fit to employ you for sixteen years on a programme designed for the pleasure and edification of the young, the men and women of tomorrow, my friends, in their most formative years, the years in which the seeds of hatred, of corruption are, alas, most easily sown. It follows from this that the British Broadcasting Corporation considers you a responsible man. Do you agree with the Corporation? Do you consider yourself responsible?'

'Yes, sir, I like to think I am.'

'There is no need to be modest here, you know. Would you consider yourself a moral man?'

'I hope so.'

'Kindly confine your answers to yes and no,' snapped Ammons, losing his smile for a moment. He hated this English incapacity to think highly of oneself in public when it was most urgently needed.

'I would like to be a moral man, sir.'

'You don't consider yourself immoral, do you?'

'Oh, no, sir,' said Edwin, horrified.

'Very well then. Would you, a moral, responsible man, knowingly take a flat above that of a known woman of the night?'

'Woman of the night, sir?'

'Prostitute,' barked Ammons.

'Oh, no.'

'How long have you been in residence at your address?'

'Three years, sir.'

'And Mrs Sidney was living there when you moved in?'

'Yes, sir.'

'It stands to reason, therefore, that she gave no appearance of being a woman who lived by commercializing her body, or you would not have stayed?'

'No, sir, I don't think I would.'

'And in the three years, the suspicion never entered your mind that she might have belonged to the world's oldest profession?'

'The world's oldest what, sir? I didn't catch that.'

'That she was a . . . a prostitute,' Ammons practically shouted. He detested having the elegance of his delivery frustrated by stupidity. He glanced at Sir Cleverdon, who smiled grimly.

'No, sir, I didn't know.'

'But you do know now, is that it?'

'I've been told.'

'Told? By whom?'

'The police.'

There was a stir. Ammons looked at the jury. 'An allegation, a slur on the character of a woman who is not here to defend herself has been cooked up callously by the police, eager for a quick conviction, whereas a responsible, a moral man, living in the closest possible proximity to the deceased, noticed no sign of his neighbour's immoral practices over a span of three years, of thirty-six months, of well nigh a thousand days!'

Sir Cleverdon objected. Mr Ammons's job was to cross-examine the witness, not to make speeches to the jury.

The judge upheld the objection, and Mr Ammons apologized without contrition.

'Take a good look at the accused. I suggest to you that you have never seen him before.'

'I couldn't swear it.'

'Would you call the face of the accused a distinctive one?'

'I wouldn't know how to answer that, sir.'

'Wouldn't you? Then I will tell you. You would answer it by a yes or a no.'

'I don't like passing personal remarks about people's faces, sir. After all they can't help the faces they are born with.'

The judge answered Ammons's mute appeal with a rap of the gavel.

'That does not seem to me a very fruitful line of country to explore, Mr Ammons,' said the judge.

'I only want to establish the fact that the accused had never been seen before by Mr Applecote, m'lud.'

'The witness has already said that he could not swear to it. Since he is under oath, we must accept his answer at its face value. He may have seen the accused, for all he knows.'

'And I may not,' said Edwin recklessly.

'I beg your pardon?'

Now even the judge was beginning to become a little rattled. His mouth looked as though there were stitches through it.

'You see, my lord,' said Edwin, 'I may have seen Mr Ahoe's face on a bus, or in the street. It certainly looks familiar, and yet it may be just that I have seen a face very much like it somewhere or other.'

'We are not here to test your memory for human physiognomy,' said the judge acidly. 'Perhaps, with Mr Ammons's permission, I may be allowed to ask you whether you actually saw the accused entering the deceased's place of residence at any time.'

'I may have done, for all I know.'

'And you may not. Very well, proceed,' muttered the judge with a huge sigh. 'The answer is no.'

'Well—'

'That's enough of that,' said the judge. 'We are wasting time.'

'Did you ever speak to Mrs Sidney?' Mr Ammons resumed.

'Yes, sir. Never much more than a good morning or a good day.'

'Would you describe her as a pleasant, well-spoken person?'

'Yes, sir. Very pleasant. And well-spoken. Her use of language was a little common perhaps, but that's not for me to say.'

'How can a person be well-spoken and common at the same time?' rasped the judge.

'It is difficult, I admit, sir. I don't like speaking ill of people. It's not my place.'

'It is your place to tell us what you know, and not to indulge in niceties here. Now, was she, in your opinion, well-spoken or vulgar?' The judge hated grey as much as he loved black and white.

'She was well-spoken, I would say.'

'Very well. Proceed.'

'With a tendency towards vulgarity.'

The judge threw up his hands.

Edwin added quickly, 'I don't think she could help it, you see.'

'She had none of the traits you would associate with her alleged profession, had she?' asked Mr Ammons. 'No excessive paint, no perfume, no high heels or black stockings or the like?'

'Well, she used a very strong perfume, sir, which I could smell upstairs.'

'Are you suggesting that her perfume penetrated through the floorboards and the carpeting?'

'Oh, yes, sir, it gave me headaches. I complained once or twice, in a polite way.'

'Did you complain orally?'

'No. Every time I went down, I could hear through the door that she had company. When she hadn't got company, she was out.'

'You mean you listened at her door?'

'Oh, no, sir, you could hear their voices halfway up the stairs.'

'Did you listen to the conversations halfway up the stairs?'

'No, sir, I only heard the conversations, I never listened. It wouldn't have been right. And it wasn't always conversation. Sometimes it was just the radio and some furniture-moving sounds.'

Ammons cleared his throat. 'I see. How did you transmit your messages of complaint if you didn't do it orally?'

'I wrote notes, which I pushed under her door.'

'Were they ever answered?'

'Never. Except—' Edwin stopped.

'Yes?'

'Once the door opened when I had just pushed my message under it.'

'Who appeared?'

'A gentleman.'

'A gentleman? How was he dressed?'

'In an undervest.'

'And?'

'That's all.'

Mr Ammons faltered. 'Do you mean to tell this Court that Mrs Sidney's door was opened by a man dressed in nothing but an undervest?'

'He may have had socks on, I can't remember.'

'No further questions.'

Sir Cleverdon rose, his eyebrows arched in triumph.

'With your lordship's permission, I would like to ask the witness a few more questions.'

'Not too many, I hope. Proceed.'

'Do you remember the face of this man or gentleman, if you prefer it. Would you recognize it again?'

'Well, he was of medium height, dark, fair skin.'

'Did he look at all like the accused?'

'Yes, now that you mention it, very much, but I could never swear it was him.'

There was some excitement in court, and Ahoe looked at Edwin with sheer hatred.

'And what did this man say to you?'

'I didn't understand what he said to me, but it sounded like—' And here Edwin spoke two words which are never used in any society. There was a gasp in court, a girl giggled, an elderly man shouted something incomprehensible, and the judge demanded order.

'We may see from this the degree of refinement which the

friends of your well-spoken neighbour were wont to reach,'
said Sir Cleverdon.

'What does it mean?' asked Edwin, sick at heart.

'Never mind,' said Sir Cleverdon, 'but I would advise
you not to use it as an expletive in civilian life, however
popular it may be in the Armed Forces.' And then he
added, to put Edwin out of his misery, 'It is a way of saying
please go away.' (Laughter.)

When silence had been re-established, Sir Cleverdon
went on, 'When did this occur?'

'About eleven o'clock in the morning.'

'But when?'

'Oh.' Edwin had not recovered from his shock. 'On the
morning of the murder.'

There was consternation. In the previous testimony,
Ahoe, who was a truck driver, had freely admitted knowing
Mrs Sidney as a casual acquaintance, but had said that he
was with his sister in Islington from nine in the morning
of the day of the murder until after the murder. His sister
had confirmed his alibi.

'Are you sure of this? On the 7th July?'

'I don't remember the date, but it was that day. I was on
my way to work.'

'What time did you leave for work?'

'About eleven.'

'Don't you know the precise time of your departure?'

'About eleven.'

'Do you mean to tell this Court that you don't know
what time you leave for work?'

Edwin began to falter. This was the last straw.

'Do people usually know exactly the time they leave for
work?'

'Yes,' snapped Sir Cleverdon.

Was he alone in the world, a freak after all? The rabbits
could never share this terrible experience with him. How

long could he stand this nightmarish room, which seemed to be full of people who knew exactly what they were doing at all hours of the day, and even knew what others should be doing.

'About eleven,' he heard his voice saying.

'What time are you due at the B.B.C.?'

'Eleven o'clock.'

'Do you mean you leave at about eleven to reach a destination halfway across town at the same hour?'

'I was late that day.'

'What time did you arrive?'

'Some time after eleven.'

'How long after eleven?'

'About ten-past . . . a quarter-past.'

'How long does it take you to get from home to the B.B.C.?'

'About twenty minutes.'

'So it is logical to suppose that you left home between five and ten to eleven?'

'I suppose so.'

'Why couldn't you have told me that at the outset?'

'Why?' Edwin blurted. 'Because I have sworn to tell the truth and nothing but the truth, and I was wrong to swear it.'

'What was that?' asked the judge.

'I don't know the truth,' he cried, wide-eyed. 'I know I should know exactly about everything, but I don't. I don't know what time I left home, and even if I knew it to the minute, I probably wouldn't know it to the second, and if I couldn't tell you everything, in the minutest detail, I wouldn't be telling you the truth.'

'You must speak up,' said the judge.

Funny, Edwin thought he had been shouting. Now it appeared he had been muttering all this to himself. He shook his head violently from side to side, closing his eyes, and saw no clearer when he opened them again.

Sir Cleverdon was looking at him intensely, an eagle. So was the judge, a vulture, and Mr Ammons, a mole.

'In any case, you left home after half-past ten in the morning?'

'I must have done.'

'Did you return home again before seven o'clock?'

'Yes, I think so.'

'You think so.'

'Please don't speak so quickly.'

'You must speak up,' said the judge.

With a superhuman effort, Edwin pulled himself together.

'The programme goes on the air at three-fifteen,' he said. 'Three-fifteen sharp. It lasts till three-forty-five.'

'What did you do after it was over?'

'I returned home to make myself a cup of tea.'

'Straight away?'

'Yes.'

'So we can assume that you arrived home between four and four-fifteen?'

'I suppose so.'

'What do you mean, you suppose so? It stands to reason, doesn't it?'

'If you say so, sir.'

'I do. How long did you stay at home?'

'Long enough to make a cup of tea and eat a scone. I had one scone, with margarine and raspberry jam. Then I washed up, dried the dishes, put them in the cupboard, and left for the zoo.'

'So, that might have taken another quarter of an hour?'

'I don't know.'

'Are you an exceptionally slow eater?'

'I don't know.'

'It really is extraordinary that there are people who go through life with no knowledge of when they do what they do or indeed how they do it. Now, concentrate if you will. During your visit to your flat in order to have your cup of tea, was there any evidence of the man's continued presence in Mrs Sidney's flat?'

'I heard voices.'

'Voices?'

'A man was shouting. The radio was on, playing dance music. There was a noise like glass breaking.'

'Did you recognize the voice as being the same as the one which had uttered that filthy expletive to your face?'

'I can't tell. It may have been, it may not.'

'Did you hear any of the words this voice uttered?'

'Yes. No, I daren't say them, for fear they may, be immodest.'

'I instruct you to tell us what you heard,' said the judge, leaning forward, 'and speak up.'

'I heard something like – one more crack, or clack out of you, and I will mash you – something like that.'

'That was the man talking?'

'Yes, is it very terrible? I remember that because I didn't understand it.'

'Did you hear her voice?'

'No, just her laugh. I kept hearing her laugh, right up to the time I left.'

'And what did you think when you heard the glass break?'

'I thought someone had dropped a glass.'

'Was it not a more violent sound than that? Was it not the sound of a glass which had been thrown rather than dropped?'

'What would be the point of that?'

'A glass can injure if it is thrown hard enough and hits its target.'

'I've never heard of anyone doing that.'

'Speak up,' said the judge.

'Now, when you left to go to the zoo,' asked Sir Cleverdon intensely, 'did you see a vehicle parked outside the house?'

'I don't remember.'

'A six-wheeled truck?'

'I don't know.'

'You noticed no vehicle at all?'

'Oh, I do remember some boys playing cricket in the street. The ball rolled under a car, and one of the boys went underneath to get it. I told him to be careful, as it was dangerous, and I looked into the driving compartment to make sure that the driver wasn't there.'

'How old was the boy?'

'About ten, twelve, fourteen perhaps. I'm not very good at the ages of children.'

'If he was playing cricket, he was presumably over six.'

'Oh, I think so, he was smoking.'

'Smoking? You said it was a car. Would a boy of an age to smoke find it easy to clamber under a modern car?'

'No, it must have been bigger than a car.'

'Did you have to stoop in order to look into the driving compartment?'

'No, I had to stand on tiptoe.'

'Stand on tiptoe? Unless the car was built before 1910, I suggest it was a truck – a grey Leyland truck, perhaps, with the name of the Hiscox Brothers of Hemel Hempstead in white letters on the door?'

Ammons objected to the form of the question. Sir Cleverdon withdrew the question, but no one could deny that he had asked it.

'I do remember something about it,' Edwin volunteered, his hand over his forehead.

Ahoe tensed visibly.

'Speak louder,' commanded the judge.

'I remember . . . there was a picture . . . a transfer I suppose it was . . . of a young lady rather immodestly dressed in a bathing costume . . . holding a coloured ball . . . it was stuck on the window the drivers have to look through to see the road . . . the windscreen, is it? I remember wondering how the police could tolerate such a thing, placed as it was, in the line of vision, and rather disgustingly suggestive.'

Although this was quite inconclusive as evidence, Ahoe evidently thought he had fallen into a trap, and being a man of short and vitriolic temper, he rose to his feet and yelled a repulsive phrase at Edwin, which Edwin mercifully didn't understand.

Sir Cleverdon threw down his papers dramatically. Ammons muttered, 'No further questions'.

The judge looked straight at Edwin and said, in the crackling tones of a boot on autumn leaves, 'If it should ever fall to your lot to give evidence again, I strongly advise you to be more observant and also more coherent. Today you initially gave the deceased a rosy and innocuous character, and then, under cross-examination, you proceeded to attribute to her a character so different that it is hard not to suspect you of mendacious intentions at the outset. I do not believe this is so, since you are clearly a man who is not used to giving evidence, and who sincerely believes that a person should be accorded the benefit of the doubt. But a benefit of the doubt is one thing, and a total blindness to the facts is another. It leads to dangerous evidence, which might, if not subjected to the most stringent methods of our legal system, even entail miscarriage of justice. I urge you to reflect on what I have said, since your evidence here today has been, in all my experience, the most misleading and the most illogical. Next witness, please.'

Edwin was not the key witness by any means. Ahoe's

sister, on re-examination, broke down and confessed that
her alibi had been a lie. The truck had been over twenty-
four hours overdue, and the police found letters and finger-
prints which eventually sent Ahoe to prison for life.

But Ahoe was not the only one whose mode of living was
affected by this case. Edwin could no longer go home. He
stayed on in the hotel, taking care to lock the door on every
occasion. He bought a little book, and carefully inscribed
the exact minute he left for work and the exact moment he
arrived for work. As he sat in the bus, his eye scanned the
road for anything suspicious or noteworthy. His perception
was unnecessarily acute, and his manner had become
curiously abrupt.

At work, he would greet his old friend Miss Alsop by
saying things he had never said before. 'Good morning,
Miss Alsop, you are wearing green, I see. Green tweed, is
it? And a cameo depicting the head of a Georgian lady in
profile. Shoes? Brown brogues, lisle stockings. Thank you.
That will be all for the moment.' And he would note all
these details in his book. Miss Butler was subjected to the
same strange treatment, and he would even stop singing
the middle of his nursery rhymes, not because he had for-
gotten the lines, but because he suddenly noticed as he sang
that the studio clock did not tally to the minute with the
watch on his wrist. Only when playing Siegfried the Rabbit
was he entirely his old self, tender, whimsical and slightly
tragic.

Miss Butler tried valiantly to understand his problem.
'Do you never go to the zoo as you used to?' she asked
kindly.

A sly look came into his eye. 'Oh, no,' he answered,
'animals can't talk. If anything were to happen to me there,
they could never give evidence.'

'What could happen to you?'

'Murder,' said Edwin, unmoved.

'Murder? Who would want to murder you?'

'There are millions of people in London,' Edwin said evasively, 'but they'd never get away with it, not now. Do you know, when I go home at night, I lock the door and write out on a piece of paper who I am and what I do, addressed to whom it may concern, and I hide it under the mattress. I outline all my movements for that day, whom I have talked to and what we talked about. You, Miss Butler, will be on it tonight, and so will our conversation.' He glanced at his watch. 'It is four-oh-eight.'

'But why do you do this, Mr Applecote?' asked Miss Butler, beginning to feel distinctly uncomfortable.

'To classify the evidence, Miss Butler. I don't know whether you've ever given evidence, but it must be clear and audible. I don't know whether you've noticed it, but I'm training myself to speak in a rather louder voice.'

'The engineers have noticed it. You're giving them a very bad time.'

Edwin laughed. 'You see, by putting the paper under the mattress, the police would discover it, but no murderer would have the presence of mind to look there.' He frowned uncertainly. 'Or perhaps he would, perhaps I'd better put it somewhere else?'

It was with genuine regret that the Children's Broadcasts Department were forced to say good-bye to Edwin Applecote, but his nursery rhymes were becoming really too erratic, and his behaviour more and more disconcerting. With unconscious cruelty, they gave him a beautifully inscribed clock as a farewell present. No two clocks ever tell precisely the same time for long, and Edwin was to spend many harassed hours checking watch and clock, and trying to find which one of them was correct.

Inspector McGlashan waited in the anteroom to see Dr Feindienst, a large cardboard box under his arm.

Eventually the doctor entered the room, and the two men shook hands.

'How is he?' asked McGlashan.

'He's a dear little fellow,' said Dr Feindienst, with a light Austrian accent. 'Quite harmless, and no trouble, not like some of them, violent paranoiacs and so on. You wish to see him?'

'May I?'

'Of course, follow me.'

'May I leave this packet here?'

'Surely.'

As they walked down the corridor, Dr Feindienst said, 'Our main problem is to keep him quiet. He is so intensely observant that he exhausts himself by noticing everything and by noting it down.'

McGlashan entered Edwin's room. The blinds were drawn.

'Remember me, McGlashan?'

'Certainly I do, the German shepherd.'

'Eh?'

Edwin was more than cordial. 'Please sit down, Inspector. Well, you'll never catch me napping again. They draw the blinds to keep me quiet, but when they're gone, I peep out. I was peeping out when I heard you coming down the corridor. You nearly caught me at it, but not quite.'

'What have you been doing?' asked the inspector. He hardly expected the answer he got.

'Me? I'll tell you. I woke up at six-thirty-seven, washed from six-thirty-nine to six-fifty-one, brushed my teeth at six-fifty-two, had breakfast consisting of a boiled egg, from New Zealand it was, said so on the shell, tea, two rolls and butter, with one lump of sugar in the tea. This took from precisely seven-oh-nine to seven-twenty-one. I read the paper, the *News Chronicle*, second edition, from seven-thirteen, when I picked it up, to seven-twenty-nine, when I put it down. Since then, I have been here in my room, except for a short walk. I left at ten-nineteen and returned at ten-forty-six. It was ten-fifty-seven when you stepped into the room. Incidentally, Inspector, what is the time on your watch?'

'Eleven sharp.'

'You're almost a minute fast.'

'Oh, thanks.' McGlashan pretended to adjust his watch.

'I say, if there should be a crime committed across the way,' Edwin whispered, indicating the window with his finger, 'at No. 18, a blue Austin station wagon pulled up there at nine-forty-one, and it's been there ever since. The number is BXC 715.'

'Thank you very much,' said McGlashan sadly, pretending to write the number down. 'When we catch him, it'll be thanks to you.'

There was a shy pause, during which McGlashan tried to hypnotize him back to sanity.

'Don't you miss your rabbits?' he said at length.

'No,' answered Edwin, 'they're happy where they are. They don't have the problems we have.'

'Perhaps they do, but we just don't understand their language.'

'Yes, perhaps they do,' said Edwin, with a noncommittal sigh.

'And don't you miss the B.B.C.?'

'Not now that I'm doing really important work, collecting evidence.'

'They miss you.'

'Who?'

'The children.'

'I've no time for children now. This is a man's world. You mustn't be too gentle, mustn't be blind to the facts.' He gave this quote from the judge a fearful emphasis.

Back in the office, Dr Feindienst asked, 'How did you find him?'

'Damn the legal profession,' said McGlashan with venom. 'What do they do? For the purposes of argument they take a completely extraordinary event, full of extraordinary and perverted aspects, and make it sound ordinary and natural. Why should a little fellow like that know all the horrible uses to which life is put by those who take it for granted? Why shouldn't he have the right to be naïve and simple. They convicted a murderer and they sent a witness off his head. That's called justice. And where are they now? In their clubs thinking of ways to make our job impossible, while that poor little bastard is in here, thinking up a lot of evidence he'll never be called on to give. It makes me sick.'

Dr Feindienst smiled. 'You sound as if you're ready to occupy one of our padded cells.'

McGlashan leaned forward conspiratorially. 'I'll tell you something, Doctor; that little fellow had something, and I'm not making this up, and I didn't get it out of my own head. I got it from my girl, aged five. I went up to say good night to her at bedtime yesterday, and she looked up at me and asked, "Daddy, why's Siegfried the Rabbit got a different voice now?" By god, Doctor, I could have told her. I could have told her, and I will one day.'

'Well, who knows, he may be able to return in a year or two.'

McGlashan shook his head. 'You know as well as I do that isn't true, Doctor. They hurt him too much out there. He can't take it. And all I say is, things should be arranged so he can take it.'

The doctor sighed. 'It's a cruel world, Inspector. Both our professions should tell us that.'

'Cruel?' said McGlashan. 'It's filthy. Filthy. And often

it's those who look the cleanest who are the filthiest. Those with responsibilities.'

McGlashan picked up his package carefully and went to the door. Before going out, he turned and said, 'We don't have to complain. We can look after ourselves.' With a strange delicacy he looked at the box he was carrying. 'I had brought him a present, but I'd better not give it him, though, after our conversation. I'll give it to my girl.'

'What is it?' asked Dr Feindienst.

McGlashan poked a piece of protruding lettuce back into the box and said softly, 'A rabbit.'

# A PLACE IN THE SHADE

Most modern guidebooks on Spain hardly mention Alcañon de la Sagrada Orden; in older ones, its name does not appear at all. And yet, the frequent discovery of Roman coins beneath its soil and a rich treasure of amphorae in its rocky waters testify to the fact that it is one of the oldest villages on the Iberian peninsula. It is not as beautiful or as dramatic as some Andalusian pueblos, but it is unspoiled and dignified.

The Church of La Sagrada Orden is by no means an architectural gem, and the interior is spoiled by some religious pictures of quite frightening sentimentality, ranging from the false Murillo to the Victorian. A vast Virgin Mary, seemingly made of marzipan, with crystal tears embedded in the rosy cheeks, dominates the body of the building as she sits, doll-like, behind glass, in a startling baroque sunburst. Typically, this outsize piece of devotional saccharin is the pride and joy of the village, and it is even said that the crystal tears miraculously turned to water during the last days of the siege of the Alcazar.

There are one or two splendid houses tucked away in side streets, including the headquarters of the local Caïd, dating from the days of the Moorish Caliphate, and a statue of the village's proudest son, Juan Rodriguez de la Jara, stands copper-green under the trees of the main square.

According to the description of this intolerant-looking hidalgo on the base of his statue, he advanced into Arizona, driving from where Tucson stands today north past Phoenix to Reno, where he died of some local plague, his last words being, '*Por España y por Alcañon.*'

Perhaps the most remarkable feature of the village, however, is its bull ring, which dates from roughly the same time as the one in Ronda and can therefore lay claim to being among the oldest in Spain. White and squat, with weeds growing patchily on its sand, it seems dangerously intimate for such a sport. The words *Sol* and *Sombra* are still visible on the dirty wall although the black paint has faded and flaked away, and the arena itself is remarkable because there is no advertisement of any sort, no reminder of a particularly delectable sherry or cognac to desecrate the functional purpose of the ancient edifice.

Although for years past the arena has been used only occasionally, the odour of animals still permeates it, just as the pungent smell of ancient urine still floats unhealthily around the public entrances, meeting places for parliaments of flies.

From the days of the Conquistador, Juan Rodriguez de la Jara until the end of World War II, Alcañon vegetated comfortably in its poverty and pride. Even the Civil War did not shake it out of its dream of glory, since it passed to the advancing troops of General Franco with only two casualties. In 1940, however, the rot set in when the great English poet, Oliver Still, decided to retire there. He was one of those men whose reputations increase the less they write. A slim volume of verse published in 1912 attracted some attention, and the agony of waiting for a second volume gradually turned it into extravagant adulation. By the time a very short novel appeared in 1925, he was known the world over. A third book, some eighty pages long, crept into print in the late thirties and made of him a demigod. Now he was a familiar figure, with his riot of grey hair and his characteristic turtle-neck jersey, which looked as though it had been knitted years ago for the gallant lifeboatmen by some half-blind old lady and which he wore defiantly, regardless of the climate.

In 1948, he produced a few pieces of mysterious, contorted poetry, bursting with rocky metrical variation and
so dense as to be barely readable at a normal pace, entitled *Recuerdos de Alcañon*. These unventilated phrases, a
kind of lyrical *foie gras*, a dense paste of verbless images,
were hailed as remarkable, and what Dr Schweitzer did for
Lambaréné, Oliver Still did for Alcañon. The village became a place of pilgrimage, and there was invariably a
Swedish journalist in the vicinity, camera at the ready, pre-
cariously hidden among the rocks to capture some unique
and candid mood in the great man, while the wife waited
patiently in a car decorated with flags and messages of
goodwill.

Gradually Oliver Still began to acquire a rival, as the
great wave of Americans in search of ancient verities and
noble savages began to break across Europe and as the
sport of the *corrida* beckoned the sophisticates with its promise of gaunt and terrible simplicity.

The mayor of the village, Señor Ramón de Villaseca, who
could trace his family back to a mistress of the great de la
Jara without any difficulty at all, saw the menace growing
and determined to meet it with a cool and arrogant eye.

He disliked everything about Oliver Still, the poetry, the
man, and the kind of interest he inspired. First of all, Still
roved over the landscape wrapped in distant and impene-
trable thoughts, a gnarled walking-stick in his hand and an
old Boy Scout rucksack on his back, smoking a pipe from
which clouds of sickly smoke vomited, too deeply lost in
his private world to acknowledge either a stray courtesy or
his wife, who trotted behind him, a tragic figure. It had
been noticed that the local dogs, who were of one accord
unreasonably ferocious, barking at cars and biting the tyres,
cringed guiltily when they saw him, and this quickly gave
him a local reputation for subtle, indefinable evil.

The pilgrims did not improve matters, with their air of

conspiracy and their incessant questioning of the villagers. They seemed to regard the poet with the kind of devotion which was to Señor de Villaseca obscene when lavished on any target smaller than God himself. The fact that Still avoided all publicity assiduously, and did his best to discourage his disciples by ignoring them completely, failed to endear him to the mayor.

'First of all, it is unnatural for one man to inspire such worship in others. Secondly, once he has inspired it, it is equally unnatural for him to reject it,' he once said to Sergeant Cabrera, of the Guardia Civil.

'It is a case of two minuses making a plus,' Sergeant Cabrera had answered penetratingly.

'Two minuses making a plus? Since when?'

'Since Aristophanes.'

'Not in Spain, thank god. Spain is the one country where Catholic order still prevails and where two minuses still make two minuses.'

Sergeant Cabrera was forced to agree, more out of patriotism than conviction.

Señor de Villaseca wrote poetry himself, ornate stuff of meticulous rhyme and scansion, fired by the unapproachable qualities of Calderón but tempered by a *fin de siècle* heart and a penchant for the lachrymose. These poems had never been published, but they had been recited frequently on various civic occasions and, owing to their lofty patriotic sentiments intertwined with sonorous references to the moon, roses, the heart, the soul, jasmine, and the state of motherhood, their effect had been immediate and tumultuous. At the same time the verses of Oliver Still, translated into Spanish in a slim volume propagated by the cultural agency of the British Government, induced overt hostility when Señor de Villaseca read them aloud to a select body of local intelligentsia.

The priest, Don Evaristo, was the most inclined to be

charitable, but then sleep had overtaken him before eight lines had been recited.

'It is to be presumed,' he said, his stout face bathed in a glow of universal brotherhood, 'it is to be presumed that some of the beauty and even some of the meaning of the original has become waylaid in translation.'

'That is out of the question,' Señor de Villaseca replied, 'since the expressiveness, the plastic and emotional content of the Spanish language, more than compensates for any loss which may occur.'

'Are you suggesting that it is a positive advantage for a Chinese thought to be transplanted many thousands of kilometres for the sole purpose of enjoying the privilege of being expressed in Castilian?' the priest asked.

'Certainly,' said Señor de Villaseca calmly. 'The Chinese language is hardly an agreeable vehicle for the diffusion of any thoughts, even of Chinese ones.'

'I agree with that,' said Sergeant Cabrera. 'My brother was in Yokohama for a while.'

And so it went on, this literary discussion inclined to tease by suggesting that perhaps Señor de Villaseca would prefer to hear Mass in Spanish, the mayor replying stoutly that if the Romans had preferred Latin, that had been their loss and was probably the reason for their ultimate decline. All were agreed, however, that the works of Oliver Still were more or less meaningless and consequently an affront to the Spanish intellect. The world was a bitter place to reward such charlatanism with fame.

'You will reap your harvest in celestial pastures,' Don Evaristo consoled the mayor.

'I need no comfort,' the mayor replied stiffly. 'My own convictions and the adulation of the good townspeople are sufficient. What revolts me, however, are the disciples this poetic quack seems to engender.'

'Who are we to say that they are disciples?' asked Don Evaristo. 'Can it not be that they are mere tempters, sent to put his vanity to the test?'

'I find it even more intolerable to think that he might be worth tempting.'

'Are we not all worth tempting?'

'On such a scale?'

'Well, after all, Don Juan probably seems to us the most tempted man in history, but is that not because he invariably surrendered to temptation? Do we not all know temptation, and yet does not our religious formation lead us to resist it?'

'Perhaps,' admitted Señor de Villaseca, thinking momentarily of his own mistress.

'To which Don Juan are you referring?' asked Sergeant Cabrera, who knew his way around the family trees of royalty.

The silent war between the unheeding poet and his cabal of critics continued until the spring of 1950, when a decision by the Duchess of Torrecaliente inspired an invasion as momentous in its small way as that of the Visigoths had been many centuries before.

The duchess was a bosomy lady, half-American and half-Polish, who had in her day borne a vague resemblance to Goya's famous picture of another, more notorious duchess, painted both dressed and naked. As though to compromise between the two aspects of her illustrious predecessor, and thereby to achieve a quintessence in both similarity and subtlety, she dressed as audaciously as the natural amplitude of her frame would allow her to.

The duke was a man drained of personality by the rigours of breeding and, although he looked remarkably like a King Edward VII shrunk by some irreverent South

American Indians, he opened his mouth only to cough. He was just a fraction under five feet tall, and a grandee of Spain. Among his few achievements, perhaps the most noteworthy were that he shot one or two very small birds every season and that he sat and slept on various committees. The duchess, on whose energies he made no very stringent demands, sat on rather more committees than he and was especially active on the council of the Society for the Prevention of Cruelty to Animals. It was she who had the brilliant idea of organizing a bullfight in aid of her favourite charity, and she had succeeded in interesting two great *toreros* in her good works. Cordobano IV, celebrated everywhere for his majestic gloom and more locally for his green Pontiac convertible, one of the newest cars in the entire peninsula, had agreed to appear, as had El Chaval de Caracas, a Venezuelan matador of incredible daring who was a network of lacerations and whose face was pitted with horrible craters like the moon.

Don Jesús Gallego y Gallego, one of the most erudite of authorities on the *corrida*, then had a brain wave and suggested that instead of holding this benefit in Madrid, which had become, to use his words, 'polluted with *turistas Norteamericanos*,' it would be fitting to reopen the historic arena at Alcañon, 'part of our *patrimonio nacional*, which will make of this a Spanish occasion, an occasion on which Spanish bulls are fought by Spanish' – and he faltered in committee – 'for the purposes of my contention, I would remind you that Venezuela is part of our cultural and taurine heritage – Spanish *toreros* before Spanish spectators, for the benefit of Spanish animals.' The applause was so volcanic that the one whom many consider the greatest of living bullfighters, Rafaelito, decided there and then to come out of retirement and to wield the third sword. With tears streaming from their eyes he and Don Jesús embraced, while the committee shouted vociferously and one or two

Pekingese, at bay in the laps of their aristocratic mistresses, began barking fitfully. Rafaelito had withdrawn from the arena for the third time a few months before and was twenty-four years of age. He had recently been unsuccessfully tested for the part of the prophet Isaiah in Hollywood. He spoke no English.

The next step was for the Duchess of Torrecaliente to visit Alcañon. She travelled together with Don Jesús, Rafaelito, and a friend of hers, the Countess of Zumayor, who was half-English and half-Italian. They met Señor de Villaseca in the town hall, and after an agreeable lunch the party, joined by Don Evaristo and Sergeant Cabrera, strolled over to examine the arena. Rafaelito threw his hat on to the hot sand, took off his jacket, and, using it as a cape, performed some exquisite passes against an imaginary bull, while the others shouted, '*Ole!*'

'What atmosphere!' he cried, when he had finished his performance with a perfect kill. 'It is as though the spirits of past generations of *aficionados* were fixing me with their critical and hostile eyes. I seem to hear applause from beyond the grave.'

The duchess closed her eyes.

'Yes, yes, now I hear it, too,' she said.

'It would be an insensitive man who did not hear it,' added Señor de Villaseca.

'What you are probably hearing is the women beating their washing against the side of the bridge,' said Sergeant Cabrera.

Don Jesús cleared his throat. 'It will be a really classical *corrida*. The cream of society will be present. Somehow we must safeguard the purity of our national festival by attempting to exclude all foreigners.'

'No foreigners ever come here,' said Señor de Villaseca, 'with the exception of journalists to interview the English mountebank, Señor Still.'

Rafaelito interrupted. 'Since this is a very special *corrida* in which I am to appear, I think there should be a *rejoneador*, as a kind of hors d'œuvre to the main event.'

'You already have Cordobano IV and El Chaval as hors d'œuvres,' said Don Jesús.

Rafaelito scowled. 'Inadequate,' he replied. 'Cordobano has no style, no passion, and no courage. As for El Chaval, he is a stunt man, a wall-of-death rider. It needs a *rejoneador* to begin the thing in style, a horseman. What could be more appropriate to the cause for which we are appealing than a man fighting a bull on horseback?'

The duchess and the countess were inclined to agree.

'The horse is such a graceful animal,' the countess observed.

Señor de Villaseca's eyes glowed. 'As mayor of this ancient town,' he said, 'would it not be appropriate if I began the proceedings?'

'For heaven's sake, be careful,' Don Evaristo pleaded.

'We know that you are knowledgeable in the matter of tauromachy,' Don Jesús said, 'but have you ever fought a bull on horseback before?'

'Frequently. I am the best horseman in Andalusia,' snapped Señor de Villaseca with as much modesty as he could muster. 'My filly, Paloma, knows no fear, and she is trained in the most elaborate of *haute école* methods. Her mother was a Pippizander.'

'Her father was a horse,' said Sergeant Cabrera, 'that I know well. Obrador.'

Don Jesús looked doubtful and lit a huge cigar.

'What could be more in the tradition of our festival than that the Alcalde himself should open it?' said Rafaelito. 'Remember, it is a popular festival, and its roots are deep in the soil of our country. It is only in recent years, since Belmonte and Joselito, that it has acquired its elegance, its nobility. Its origins are raucous, popular, rough. When this ring was built, it was still a test of strength and stamina rather than the art it is today. What could be more fitting than that a tribute be paid to the glorious past of Alcañon by its first citizen, an amateur, a Spaniard of mettle, who compensates in sheer arrogance what he may lack in style.'

Señor de Villaseca looked at Rafaelito with loathing, since he intended to have immaculate style, but he was silent, because the great man was evidently swaying opinion. Don Jesús was still a little lacking in enthusiasm. As they left the ring, he drew Rafaelito aside and said softly, 'What if he makes a fool of himself?'

'I rather hope he does,' smiled Rafaelito.

'What?'

'People take us for granted,' Rafaelito said, his handsome face cold and cruel. 'They think our job is easy. They expect more from us than we can give. Even a wire-dancer pretends to fall in order to emphasize the danger of his profession. We can't do that, so let someone do it for us. If he gets hurt, it will remind the crowd that bull-fighting is not a ballet but a game played with death.'

A dark cloud passed over Don Jesús's face. 'That is an atrocious hope,' he said.

'It is not the hope which is atrocious,' answered Rafaelito, 'but human nature. You remember when I was accused of having the horns of my bulls blunted?'

'Is that why you are so bitter?' asked Don Jesús. 'They had no right to accuse you of any such thing.'

'Why not,' said Rafaelito, 'since it was true?'

'I know it was,' Don Jesús replied in a dead voice.

Rafaelito smiled the smile of a man twice his age. 'Bull-fighting is no more corrupt than life,' he said.

The forthcoming *corrida* attracted great attention, and a famous impressario, Don Jacinto de Costats, decided that, in spite of the somewhat uneconomical size of the arena, a series of events could be run there on the basis of a kind of

Salzburg festival of the bulls. Don Jacinto, a hard-headed and much-travelled man from Barcelona, declared in an interview with the assembled press that he foresaw tickets being issued to cover the entire ten days. Furthermore, he said he would hire only the best performers and that the cost of seats would be on the high side to keep the event exclusive. 'It will make Madrid's Feast of San Isidro look like a tavern brawl,' he added.

So taken was Señor de Villaseca with the intoxication of appearing as a *rejoneador* that he never realized the danger of all this publicity and authorized the use of the ancient bull ring both by the charitable organization and by Don Jacinto largely because he was to appear himself. The businessman had shrewdly insinuated that perhaps the mayor would care to put in more than one appearance. After an elaborate show of reluctance, Señor de Villaseca allowed himself to be persuaded.

Soon the bills went up all over the town and in neighbouring cities. An extraordinary *corrida de toros*, it was to be, with El Famosissimo Rejoneador, Ramón de Villaseca. 10th May was the date selected, and at the same time other bills went up announcing the Feria de San Mamerto, whom someone had hurriedly raked up as patron saint of Alcañon, running from 11th to 17th May, for which the greatest swords in Spain were promised.

On the morning of the seventh, Don Jacinto de Costats was seated outside the tavern in the main square of the village talking to Cordobano IV, who had just arrived in his green Pontiac. The don was in a good mood, and his small blue eyes sparkled with pleasure and with malice.

'They do the work, clean up the ring, tear out the weeds, restore it to its original condition, and then I take over. That's what I call business.' He glanced at Cordobano IV, who was frowning, his face lit with a strange dull glow, as though storm clouds were passing behind the head of a tortured saint on a stained-glass window.

Don Jacinto followed Cordobano's gaze to a mauve Cadillac which was parked ostentatiously next to the only no-parking sign in town, at the very foot of de la Jara's statue.

'Rafaelito?' he said. 'You don't have to worry about him. He is essentially a fraud, a matinée idol, without dignity, without melancholy, without honesty.'

'I am not worried about him,' said Cordobano, 'I am worried about his Cadillac. A *torero* is no longer judged by the same pure standards as he was in the old days. Nowadays it is impossible for a *torero* who arrives at the *corrida* in a Cadillac to be a coward, even if he retreats before the bull.'

'You exaggerate.'

'Do I? Don't you think my Pontiac has helped me in my career? Before, when I used to arrive at the Plaza de Toros in a taxi, it was always my fault if the fight turned out to be indifferent. Ever since I bought my Pontiac, it has always been the bull's fault. And now here's this impudent bastard spoiling the market by arriving in a Cadillac. I tell you, Don Jacinto, it's a deliberate stab in the back, a calculatedly unfriendly act.'

'If he had to rely only on quality, he would be nowhere,' said Don Jacinto.

'You are a true friend,' replied Cordobano warmly.

Later in the day a jeep drove into the square, crammed with electrical equipment.

Judging from the driver's appearance, he was American. He was very fair, had a crewcut over a face like a depressed pillow, covered in freckles, glasses barely able to find a resting place on a tiny nose, and great white teeth protected from adolescence by dentifrice and science. His wife, seated by his side, was dark and sulky. Both wore blue jeans and T shirts.

A few minutes after their arrival, a sports car roared into the square, driven with unnecessary abandon, and squealed to an abrupt standstill beside the jeep.

'I got her up to 150 on the straight!' called the driver.

'You mean 144,' cried the exhilarated girl by his side.

'What's the difference?'

Soon all four of them were seated outside the tavern and conspiring.

Don Jacinto and Cordobano IV were still there, sipping their drinks, and with the instincts of the businessman Don Jacinto was doing his best to overhear the conversation. He spoke a little English, and after a while, detecting a note of perplexity in the discussion at the next table, he leaned over and asked if there was anything they needed. The man with the crewcut introduced himself as Bayard Bruin, Junior, and said that he and his friend, the sports car driver, Lake Linquist, and their wives were all directors of a corporation which produced ethnic records in New York. They had been to Guatemala to record the song of the Quetzal, unsuccessfully, and they had been waiting for nearly a year for a visa to go to Romania, in order to capture the sounds of the vagrant gypsies. Bayard Bruin talked big, and there was evidently a weight of inherited money behind his schemes, but he failed to reveal that none of his records had yet succeeded in hitting the market.

'Why are you here?' asked Don Jacinto.

'We are *aficionados*,' declared Bruin, seriously, 'and we hope to put out an authentic disc of the actual sounds of the *corrida* for the American market – not merely the obvious sounds, the crowd, the *paso-dobles* – but the noise of man and bull, if possible, the silences, the tensions, the conflict. Lake here does colour photography, and we hope to combine in a single exclusive album the photographs of the *corrida* and the associated sounds, selling for about thirty dollars. We have a great letter from Dali, declining to design the cover, but we feel it's a step on the right road. We may use Juan Miró instead.'

Cordobano, hearing a reference to the American market, talked rapidly to Don Jacinto in Spanish.

Don Jacinto translated into English, while the tragic face of Cordobano was lit by an eager smile.

'He wants to know if you wish to do any interviews with the *toreros* for the American market.'

'Sure.'

'He is ready to do one.' Cordobano was violently jealous of Rafaelito not only because of his popularity but because of that Hollywood test. In the confusion of all things American which exists in many simple European minds, Cordobano imagined that an interview might be halfway to a movie contract.

'Excuse my ignorance,' said Bruin, 'but who is your friend?'

'The greatest *torero* in all Spain,' replied Don Jacinto, 'Cordobano IV.'

The girls shrieked with pleasure.

'We so admired your wonderful veronicas in Valencia,' cried Mrs Linquist.

'Alice, how about that *faena* we caught in Pamplona!' said Mrs Bruin.

Cordobano bowed gravely, a medieval knight about to enter the lists.

'Yes, how about that?' echoed Bayard, reverently.

'Greatest *faena* I ever did see,' added Lake, throwing a piece of sugar into the air and catching it again nonchalantly.

The interview was recorded that afternoon. Cordobano talked for about an hour, attacking his rivals, describing his own genius in grave and haughty tones, and expressing a great interest in the American entertainment industry. All references to the United States were promptly edited out of the tape by Bayard. He wanted his savages really noble for that ethnic trade.

The next morning the boys approached Rafaelito through Don Jesús, who attempted to throw them into the street until he heard that Cordobano had already done an interview. After a furtive discussion in whispers, Rafaelito appeared in a silk dressing-gown covered with undersized matadors and oversized bulls, and Lake promptly took more than a hundred pictures, firing like a machine-gunner. Rafaelito dismissed all other *toreros* as frivolous. Cordobano IV? A mortician trying to play Hamlet. Dominguin? Please don't mention the name in my presence, it gives me migraine. Litri? How do you spell it? Aparicio? Why don't you start from the top of the list? He ended his interview by sending personal good wishes to Colonel Darryl Zanuck and other close friends in Hollywood, but once again Bayard saw to it that the messages never reached their destination.

On the afternoon of the eighth, El Chaval and his *cuadrilla* arrived by train, a disreputable and rowdy lot, members of an equatorial beat generation. El Chaval talked English, having been brought up in the oil wells of Maracaibo, and he branded all other bullfighters as effeminate weaklings, more concerned with their physical gentility than with the raw contest. His colleagues, many of whom were as cut up as he, roared with demoniac approval whenever he slammed into his rivals, and Bayard had to hold down the sound on his tape recorder, so uncouth were their jungle noises.

Señor de Villaseca was unaware of these changes in his town, since he was away in a distant field putting his horse

through its paces. Sergeant Cabrera stood in the bushes
like a racing tout, and a not very happy tout at that. The
horse had a highly developed choreographic sense, but the
paternal strain had evidently prevailed, and while Sergeant
Cabrera played a waltz on an old horn phonograph, the
animal seemed to be permeated with the spirit of the *sequi-
dillas* and the *zapateado*, making it extremely difficult for
Señor de Villaseca to retain his arrogance, or indeed his
seat.

'Put a bull in the field as well, and you've got chaos,'
thought Sergeant Cabrera. 'In the words of the immortal
Cervantes, lose all hope, you who enter here.'

Oliver Still was also beginning to lose his composure.
As he walked through the village, he noticed that there was
no one for him to ignore, since they were all busy ignoring
him. He heard English spoken everywhere as the caravan-
sary of foreign *aficionados* streamed into town. The Rolls-
Royce of a celebrated literary agent who had never heard
of Oliver Still arrived, carrying a film star dressed subtly in
Spanish national costume in the interest of public relations.
Several parties of squeamish British Naval officers accompanied by their bloodthirsty wives came in from Gibraltar.
Two busloads of West German tourists from Düsseldorf
were joined by a group from Eindhoven and another one
from Upsala. Some professional gypsies pitched their tents
on the outskirts of the town, performing authentic flamenco
dances for exorbitant fees and playing jazz records while
waiting for customers to arrive. Dispensers of artificial
lemonade and candy floss filled every train to pull in at the
station, while a track for dodg'em cars was erected just
outside Oliver Still's window, so that his august medita-
tions were filled with the commas of lightning from the
electrified grid and the hoarse groan of the little vehicles
as adults rediscovered their lost childhood by charging into
each other inoffensively.

To put it mildly, Oliver Still was in a filthy temper.

He threw a teacup on to the track late that night, and everyone roared with good-natured laughter, believing that he had entered into the spirit of the *feria*. Someone even threw a bottle of gaseous cherryade back.

'Pack our bags,' Still barked at his wife.

'What for?'

'Trust you to ask an idiotic question. We're leaving.'

'Tonight?'

'Not tonight. As soon as bloody well possible.'

'Where are we going?'

'Greece. Greece or Japan. I'll tell you when I've made up my mind.'

'But—'

'Don't you understand plain English?'

To console himself, the great man picked up a recent edition of the *Atlantic Monthly* and read, 'Without question, Oliver Still, both as a man and as an artist, represents the last remaining example of the civilized man, the liberal humanist who is not scared of doubt, who does not need the poison of conviction as a justification for existence. As he himself says, "Is love not enough? It is a river which flows through the pasture of the human heart. What matter if we never find its source? Exploration will never alter the fact that the river is there, that the water is clear, and warm, that it cleanses, that it *is* . . ." '

'Will you be needing all your books?' asked his wife.

'Don't interrupt.'

At last the great day arrived. The military governor of the region, General Castro de Real Montijo, also known as the Wolf of the Sahara, was the president of the *corrida*. He weighed more than three hundred pounds, and his breathing was louder than his voice. At precisely six o'clock he took his place in the presidential box, leaning heavily on the arm of an exhausted Moroccan legionary. The duchess,

crowned by a white mantilla which was stretched compli-
catedly over a network of combs, making her head look
like a radar installation under a camouflage net, sat by his
side, holding her Pekingese on her knees so that it could
see the sport. The dog, grunting and grumbling adenoid-
ally, had a little black mantilla of its own, and a bull-
fighter's coat in red velvet with its name stitched on it in
gold thread. The countess sat next to the duchess. She wore
Andalusian costume, meaning that the score of dignitaries
seated immediately behind could not see the ring at all.
The duke sat next to the countess, mounted on a pyramid
of cushions, and Don Jesús, assuming the drawn mouth
and dark glasses of the professional critic, looked bored at
the end of the line.

The places in the shade were largely taken by the society
people who had travelled from Madrid and from Seville for
the occasion, but the yellow heads of the Swedish and
Dutch contingents could be plainly seen. The Germans
were busy passing beer and sausages to each other over
immense distances, and some of the ladies, frightened of
sunstroke even in the shade, had made knots at the four
corners of handkerchiefs and sat munching their endless
picnic with these unbecoming helmets on their heads. The
élite of Hollywood sat in the front row, which was aglitter
with telescopic lenses. The people, among them the Bruins
and the Linquists, sat in the sun.

Don Jesús was disgusted. Spain was too poor to dispense
with foreigners. He had done his best to exclude them, but
the dollar and the hard mark and solid krone had spoken.
The general looked at his watch, or rather he extended his
arm and the Moroccan told him the time. His rate of
breathing increased audibly as he reached for his handkerchief in his breast pocket. His medals tinkled like a Glock-
enspiel as he fumbled. Eventually he found it and, making
a supreme effort, held it aloft.

The sour trumpets sounded, a door slowly opened, and two venerable horsemen emerged, dressed from head to foot in black, with orange cockades in their hats. Like all the auxiliary horses seen in the ring, these seemed to be moving on their points, aged ballerinas giving farewell performances. They headed the procession. Behind them came the *toreros*. Cordobano's suit was of light green, the green of his Pontiac, and he strode across the arena oblivious of everything but his comportment, which was dignified to the point of absurdity.

Rafaelito, dressed in a mauve which exactly matched his Cadillac, was smiling in an icily inviting way to his public, while El Chaval seemed frankly out of place in such company, wearing a suit the colour of old ivory, which, judging from the ill-disguised patches and rents, had seen more than its ration of *corridas*. He grinned sheepishly under a montera several sizes too large. Behind them came Señor de Villaseca, who spent most of his time looking nervously over his shoulder, since his horse was giving him trouble already and seemed to prefer walking backwards. The picadors followed, like Sancho Panzas on mounts borrowed from Don Quixote. After them, the team of mules, gaily caparisoned to tug the carcasses from the arena, and an ancient truck, rented from the street-cleaning services of a neighbouring township, its rusty sprinklers dropping two parallel tracks of water on the sand.

The two *alguacils* bowed to the president, sweeping their hats aside, and then galloped stiffly in a great arc, while the matadors bowed in their turn to the president, who responded by nodding. As he did so, the blood was squeezed out of his chins, which became white. The matadors then exchanged their *capotes de paseo* for their capes, and waited. One of the *alguacils* cantered back, received the order to proceed from the president, and then handed the key to the keeper of the gate leading to the *toril*. As he was doing this, Señor de Villaseca reappeared, noble as an equestrian statue if not quite as passive, his filly showing the whites of its eyes in a decidedly disconcerting manner.

Before anyone realized it, the *toril* gate was open and shut, and one of the ferocious bulls of Doña Concepción Morales Prado, from Albacete, stood in the sun, perplexed yet confident. A gasp of expectancy rose from the crowd. Attracted by vague movements in the crowd, the bull moved forward cautiously and was observed to have a slight limp.

'*Fuera, fuera!*' roared the spectators, 'away with it! Another bull!'

Señor de Villaseca studied his adversary without much enthusiasm, since he could not induce his horse to move. Just then, on a signal, the band began a *paso-doble*. The horse, which had been trained to the sounds of a distant phonograph and which had had no opportunities in its short life for much musical appreciation, suddenly shot forward at a terrific clip and headed straight for the bull. A cry of enthusiasm went up. So precipitate was Señor de Villaseca's advance that the bull, unable readily to identify the character of the missile heading in its direction, retreated nervously.

'What arrogance!' cried the duchess, and even the small dog's eyes seemed to bulge with admiration. For one exquisite moment, the townsfolk were really proud of their mayor. Even Rafaelito wondered for a second whether he had not made a terrible mistake. The doubt was short-lived, however, because at one and the same time the bull realized that the black blur which had flashed across its field of vision was nothing more than a man on a horse, and the horse realized that the static obstruction in the middle of the arena was something as horrible as a bull.

Señor de Villaseca had very little influence on the chase

which followed, except that, to his credit, he managed to stay in the saddle. The bull apparently had a one-track mind and a surprising wind, whereas the horse was a singularly stupid strategist and even tried to leave the ring by pawing the barrier.

Twice the bull's horns became enmeshed in the horse's tail, while the crowd was too spellbound to hiss. At last the bull stopped and stood in the bright sunlight, panting. A volcano of booing erupted. Señor de Villaseca, in a fury, managed to bring the horse to a standstill at the other side of the ring. Grimly he took a couple of *banderillas* from his helpers in the *callejón* and spurred the wretched animal with all the violence born of his humiliation. Grudgingly it moved sideways to the centre of the ring.

'Toro!' he cried, so that all Spain could hear.

'Toro!' he cried again, Roland's trumpet-call at Roncesvalles, the Christian challenge to the infidel.

The uproar was stilled by the magnificence of the challenge, by its indomitable will, by its grandeur. Its effect on men was immediate, but unfortunately the bull heard it too and, turning its head, saw the horse. A second later the horse saw the bull, and the degrading chase began again. To make matters worse, the mayor attempted to turn in his saddle and place his *banderillas* in the bull's back. Both fell harmlessly to the ground. Luckily the bull was a little weary, and the second chase was much shorter than the first. The booing was now mixed with laughter. Señor de Villaseca took a second lot of *banderillas* from his assistants, said some very offensive things to his mount, and coaxed it towards the puffing bull. This time his approach to his quarry was much more underhanded. He made no attempt to shout. Instead he cleverly profited from his horse's predilection for walking backwards and gave it its head, so that it neared the bull without seeing it. The bull had come to rest near a *burladero*, one of the four narrow

protected entrances in the *barrera*, and stood staring at the
chipped woodwork, its black tongue just visible.

While Señor de Villaseca was calculating his distance for
the great and triumphal assault he was still envisaging, a
long metal rod crept out over the bull's head. The rod had
a microphone on one end and Bayard Bruin, Junior, on the
other. The bull sniffed the microphone, and Bayard, his
anxious eyes just visible over the top of the *burladero*,
shouted in the hope of exciting the bull into some sort of
recordable sound. Señor de Villaseca, livid, waved to the
police, ordering them to arrest the criminal, but in doing so
he brought the horse's head round to face the bull. At the
moment that the mayor was leaning heavily to the right
side of his horse, pointing at Bayard with both *banderillas*,
the horse decided to bolt towards its left, and Señor de
Villaseca dropped like a stone on to the sand. The bull
ambled over and sniffed him, toyed with him for a moment,
and then responded to the urgent tattoo beaten on his back
by the rattan canes of the *monosabios*, turned, saw the
horse, and resumed the traditional chase.

This was enough for the president, who declared the conflict over, sent for the steers, and the bull trotted meekly
out of the arena while Señor de Villaseca wept unasham-
edly, in the arms of the good Don Evaristo, who was ready
in the *callejón* in case any extreme unction should be called
for.

'The bull didn't even kill me!' moaned the mayor.

'There's always tomorrow,' said Sergeant Cabrera in
consolation.


After a fanfare, the second bull emerged. The preliminaries
revealed it to be an impulsive and unreliable beast. Cordobano studied it grimly. It was given to sudden rushes and
equally sudden doubts. Curiously enough, its interest in the
picadors' horses was inquisitive rather than hostile. Having

had the lance dug into its back once, it was reluctant to go too near the horses a second time. The whole episode was drawn out and ugly in the extreme, the picadors being forced to chase the animal slowly towards the centre of the ring, amid shouts of derision and fury from the crowd. Eventually the fanfare announced the president's decision that the animal had had enough of this treatment, and the poker-faced picadors left the ring amid tumult. Cordobano IV walked regally towards the presidential box, where he raised his montera, permitted himself a bow of half an inch, and asked permission to kill the bull. The president blinked his approval of the idea, and Cordobano dedicated the bull to the duchess, who arched her eyebrows with a sense of the tragic, although any observer might equally guess from her expression that a drop of cold water had fallen on her back.

Slowly Cordobano walked to his selected terrain and stared at the bull. The bull moved an inch or two forward, stopped. Cordobano, his feet close together, his pelvis thrust forward defiantly, and his chin tucked down as though holding a violin in place, prepared to elevate an unpromising adversary on to the plane of tragedy if he possibly could. Just then there was an uncanny gust of wind, the first whisper of a storm, Rafaelito, smoking a cigarette in the *callejón*, looked upward and assessed the sky with a grim and expert eye. It was still blue, but far away there was a small cradle of white cloud, turning black at the edges. He grimaced.

The gust of wind had caught Cordobano's muleta and sent it back like the cloak of a galloping horseman. The bull saw the movement and ran forward to investigate. Quite near Cordobano, it stopped dead. Cordobano, the furrows of melancholy cascading down his cheeks, looked away from the bull in supreme defiance.

'Why don't you look what you're doing?' cried the Dutch tourists, who were thorough people.

The bull charged and knocked Cordobano sideways with his bulk.

'What did we tell you?' cried the Dutch, in Dutch.

'I hope they didn't give you a driving licence,' cried one man.

Cordobano tried a series of curtailed and unsatisfactory veronicas, but the bull had excellent brakes and no acceleration whatever, which made the passes extremely dangerous. There were some feeble '*oles*', exclusively from tourists, since the word sounded as though they were reminding a receding waiter that they wished milk in their coffee.

'Kill it!' cried the Spaniards, realizing that there was little to be done with such a sly animal.

Cordobano was unwilling to let it go at that, however. That Pontiac had made him the underdog, and he was eager for heroism. Ending his series of passes with a media-veronica, he walked proudly away from his adversary and took up a new position with the intention of performing some *manoletinas*, passes in which the torero turns away from the bull, with the muleta lifted above its horns as it passes. The first one was surprisingly successful and brought forth the first full-blooded '*ole*' of the afternoon. From the sudden wince on Cordobano's face it was clear, however, that something had gone wrong on the second one. What it was became immediately apparent when Cordobano turned and it was seen that the unpredictable bull, in a sudden tossing motion, had taken away the seat of Cordobano's trousers, and now, conscious of some annoyance, it was strolling around the ring trying to shake the piece of green silk off its horn.

'How charmingly indecent!' cried the duchess, lifting a lorgnette to her eyes.

'He really is built like a Greek god,' whispered the countess. Continued arrogance was difficult for poor Cordobano. The Spanish public was willing to overlook a bare bottom if the contest was noble, but the Northern delegations, with a more Breughelesque sense of impropriety, roared with uncontrolled glee, some of the ladies mingling their fits of schoolgirl giggles with moments of elaborately offended modesty.

Every time Cordobano moved, the fragile cloth gave a little more, and the famous film star exchanged her dark glasses for ones with more powerful lenses. There was nothing for it but to kill the bull quickly, in the interests of decency, and go to the changing room. Cordobano sized up the bull, dropped his muleta. The bull advanced, and as Cordobano leaned forward to deliver the *coup de grâce*, he felt that the moment of truth had arrived not only for the bull but also for his pants. Wrapping himself in his muleta, he looked as triumphant as he dared. The kill was a fine, clean, honest one.

One witty townsman shouted to the president, 'Grant him an ear to cover himself with, for the sake of decorum.' The president grunted but awarded Cordobano nothing.

Rafaelito's bull was more athletic, running around aimlessly and angrily for a while.

'*Fuera, fuera!*' shouted the crowd, almost out of habit. These bulls seemed to have every variety of vice. The first had a physical deformity, the second was cunning, and now the third lacked concentration. It charged the horses viciously, however, unseating two picadors, but quickly lost interest in its adversaries and rushed off to find something else to attack. It chased the *banderilleros* all the way to the *burladero* and even charged the *barrera* as the crowd gasped.

Rafaelito smiled and dedicated his bull to the film star,

who threw him a rose, which he kissed ostentatiously. He placed himself far away from the bull, put a handkerchief on the ground, and stood on it. The crowd applauded. The bull saw him, lowered its head, and came forward, but a high wind suddenly blew, taking the Germans by surprise and carrying the débris of their picnic into the ring like a plague of locusts. Greasy papers which had once enclosed sausages mingled with soiled copies of Düsseldorf newspapers and tinfoil and even some handkerchiefs. A few feet away from Rafaelito, the bull found itself met by a torrent of white and silver objects, a greaseproof wrapping fixing itself to its chest like a huge postage stamp and a copy of an evening paper bearing a large picture of Chancellor Adenauer settling over one eye. Furiously the bull changed its course, leaving Rafaelito still standing on his handkerchief, isolated and unchallenged. Although weakened by the picadors, the bull charged the *barrera* and with an incredible, almost canine leap landed in the *callejón*.

There was chaos as the doctors, policemen, journalists, and priests ran helter-skelter round the narrow track, followed by Chancellor Adenauer, who was still appealing for European unity on the bull's eye. By the time the bull was lured to re-enter the arena, it was practically cleared except for the small figure of Don Evaristo, who was walking slowly in the sun, his hand grasping his side, and for Rafaelito, who was still standing on his handkerchief.

'Ho, ho!' cried Rafaelito, but the bull, which was quite close to him, evidently enjoyed long sight and saw only Don Evaristo. The crowd called for him to run, but the priest, mistaking their concern for an upsurge of religious conviction, waved back benevolently. Since the yelling increased, he turned around to see the bull rushing in his direction and, gathering up his robes, began to run.

The sight tickled the fancy of the president, who began to rock with laughter, his medals jostling each other.

'It is fitting to see a good friar turning his back on a creature with horns,' he wheezed.

'Is he in any danger?' inquired the duchess with some alarm.

The dog barked asthmatically.

'This *corrida* is becoming like ancient Rome,' said Don Jesús sarcastically. 'In the absence of competent gladiators we have to sacrifice the Christians.'

'Zigzag!' appealed the crowd.

The bull was almost on Don Evaristo when El Chaval rushed out, confusing the bull by hitting its nose with the palm of his hand. The crowd applauded the daring *quite*, and Don Evaristo fainted as soon as he reached the *callejón*. Rafaelito, who seemed to be impaled on his handkerchief, was livid and shouted insults at El Chaval for interfering with his bull. El Chaval made a rude Venezuelan gesture, which few understood, and cockily turned the bull to face Rafaelito, even pointing at his rival. The poor bull was entirely perplexed but obediently moved off towards Rafaelito. The ring was now so covered with refuse that it seemed like a field of dandelions in full bloom. Lowering its head, the bull rushed at Rafaelito, who was forced to give a little ground because the wind was now playing havoc with the muleta, wrapping it around him. After a few unsatisfactory passes, including the Rafaelitina, which is performed on the knees with the back to the bull and the muleta dropped to the ground, so that the animal turns in a slow circle around the matador, Rafaelito decided to kill it. He made four unsuccessful attempts, while the Teutonic women howled their disgust at him. No ears, no tail.

The rain began to fall as El Chaval rushed to the door of the *toril*, knelt there with his back to the gate, and smiled. 'No, no!' chanted the crowd. As the fourth bull appeared, a tremendous gust of wind carried the capote out of El Chaval's hands, and the enraged beast tossed the Venezuelan high into the air while the spectators screamed. El Chaval landed nimbly on his hands, did a spectacular somersault, and faced the bull again.

'Toro!' he yelled, in a transport of passion.

The bull went for him again, and he, armed with neither sword nor capote, worked the bull all the way across the ring by keeping just inside its turning circle, patting it on the forehead, touching its horns, teasing it. A great shout of acclaim rose from the public, but by now it was raining so hard that it was impossible to see across the arena at all. Evidently the sudden icy downpour excited the patriotism and the nostalgia of the Swedes, who began to sing a hearty Northern drinking-song in a depressing unison.

El Chaval and the bull stood like scarecrows in the ring and saw the spectators leave by the thousands. The Moroccan legionary opened a huge umbrella over his master, and the Wolf of the Sahara hobbled to shelter. Mistaking a distant motor horn for the sound of the trumpet, Sergeant Cabrera drove the old street-cleaning truck into the arena, its sprinklers turned full on to help the rain in its work of destruction. After all, he was a soldier, and nobody had countermanded his orders. The bull saw the truck and charged it, lifting the back wheels off the ground and dropping them again so hard that the half-shaft broke and the truck came to a standstill. Again and again the bull attacked the vehicle, twisting the sprinklers into grotesque shapes, so that the truck began to look like an ornamental fountain, water squirting in all directions. The bull then turned its attention on to the radiator, which it lifted like a honeycomb and threw away. Sergeant Cabrera was a veteran of the wars against the Riff, and he knew how to deal with insubordination under fire. He drew his revolver and emptied it into the bull.

The disgrace of the occasion was on every tongue. In answer to questions, Doña Concepción Morales Prado, the somewhat masculine breeder of the bulls, said, 'One does not give one's best bulls to charity.' The Duchess of Torrecaliente was nowhere to be found, since her Pekingese had caught pleurisy and she spent the evening in isolation, kneeling by its basket. (The duke had caught pneumonia the year before, and the duchess had entrained for Vichy on the very same day, to take the waters.) The film star left that evening for Cannes, accompanied by Cordobano, who blessed the bull for tearing his pants.

'She was slipping from popularity even when I was in Hollywood,' said Rafaelito bitterly.

Most deeply wounded of all, however, was Señor de Villaseca. Don Evaristo tried to console him. 'Think how truly humiliating it would have been,' he said, 'if the other displays had been magnificent, but they were not. Why, how can you sit there brooding while close friends of yours were exposed to even greater danger? It is not very charitable, my son. Why, the bull only sniffed you. I have a hoof-mark on my cassock!'

'I am not concerned about danger,' snapped Señor de Villaseca, 'but about honour!'

'There are times when honour is impossible!' cried Don Evaristo.

'In Spain?' The mayor's eyes flashed. 'It is the fault of the foreigners, *los extranjeros,* who come here polluted by dishonour and taint us.'

'We must move with the times, my child! Why, even Sergeant Cabrera had to make use of modern technology in order to dispose of the bull. Had he not had his revolver, he would be an honourable Spanish corpse by now, and I'd have dozens of relatives to console. Now I warrant his revolver is not of Spanish manufacture.'

'It is German,' said Sergeant Cabrera, 'a Mozart.'

'Precisely,' declared Don Evaristo. 'We must learn, and

not only learn, but be better. Then the foreigners will no longer patronize us and come to our country in search of the picturesque, the out of date.'

'By God and all His Angels,' cried the mayor, 'you're right! They have come to regard us exactly as the great de la Jara used to regard them. We have become *los Indios*, the quaint, the primitive, the savage. They come here to study us as though we were in a zoo. The over-sophisticated women of California come here in search of primitive men, machines for uncomplicated, elemental love-making! The men from over there come to record our peculiar habits for posterity on phonographs and on film! It is degrading!'

He took up the telephone and asked for a number in Valencia.

'What are you going to do?' demanded Don Evaristo.

'You will see.'

After two hours' delay, the number became available.

'Don Alipio Ybazoa? This is Ramón de Villaseca. After mature consideration, and whatever it may cost me in litigation, I have decided to accede to your terms.' The man on the other end seemed highly delighted.

Late that evening, Señor de Villaseca went to church. On his way, he passed the statue of de la Jara. Looking up at the green copper face, he muttered, 'You fool. What you started!'

He knelt before the miraculous Virgin and prayed.

'Blessed Virgin of Alcañon,' he said, 'see to it that we find our way in the world again, as once we did, and that we point the path of progress out to others, since our pride will not allow us to follow, but only to lead. Inspire our men of science to produce a Spanish airplane, a Spanish missile, a Spanish rocket, a Spanish artificial moon, and even if this should take time, grant that the next occasion on which Sergeant Cabrera is forced to shoot a bull, let it be with a Spanish revolver.'

*        *        *

The next evening, when the *aficionados* went to the arena, they were surprised to find notices posted around the bull ring announcing the abandonment of the *feria*. Inside, workmen were busy erecting an enormous curved screen. In place of the *corrida*, there was to be a drive-in movie show. With unconscious irony, the film selected to inaugurate this new phase in civic development was *Blood and Sand*. Señor de Villaseca looked at his handiwork with satisfaction. There was nothing to attract foreigners any more. Oliver Still had slunk off to Lemnos, one of the Greek islands, with his dishevelled dreams. The disciples would have further to travel. The town was rediscovering its dignity, its expensive place in the shade, for the price of poverty is always excessive. But it was looking forward with confidence to a more modern future. Was there a screen as large as that in all the New World?

As Señor de Villaseca stood there, proudly confident, a furious Don Jacinto strode up to him.

'Ah, there you are, you twister! I've been looking for you all day! I just want you to know that I'm suing you for ten times the amount you'll ever earn in your life.'

The mayor closed his eyes benignly and echoed the words of his great forefather.

'I did it,' he said, '*por España y por Alcañon!*'

# THE AFTERTASTE

In normal times, there was snow as far as the eye could see, snow, smooth as a marshmallow. This winter, however, there were blemishes on the clear face of the landscape. It was as though a knife had cut through a gigantic apple, only to find a family of peaceful maggots hibernating there in yellowed trenches, untidily. They were horses, men, all dead. The wind howled, whistled, died, howled again. Snowflakes drifted by, leap-frogging, scurrying, rising mysteriously as well as falling. There was a hovel in the middle of nothing, a shabby hut which seemed to have fallen on to one knee in the snowdrifts, more like a moving thing which had become bogged down than a static edifice. No discernible road led to it. It was alone.

Inside, in the semi-darkness, half-hidden under blankets, were the 603rd Mountain Division, the 346th Nibelungen SS Regiment, the 425th Special Engineer Brigade, and the 78th Italian Brigade, each represented by their last surviving member, General Leopold Reims, General Egon Freiherr Von Augenstrahl, General Rudolf Kowalka, and General Baldessare Capognoni.

They had not eaten for two days, they had not slept for three, they had not fought for a week. If the battle was still going on, they had no evidence of it. There was no gunfire, only the wind.

'I give it another ten minutes,' growled General Reims in a weak voice.

'And then what?' asked General Kowalka.

'And then I will take my life.'

'Why wait ten minutes?'

Reims threw Kowalka a look of disdain and tapped his

breast pocket. He took out an empty packet of Overstolz cigarettes, searched it for perhaps the fiftieth time, rolled it into a ball, and threw it on the floor.

General Capognoni had three cigarettes left, flat Italian ones. He had kept them for emergencies. Now he offered one to Reims from a golden *étui*.

'I don't smoke,' said Reims, not looking at Capognoni.

'I will, with pleasure,' said Kowalka.

Kowalka and Capognoni lit up. The Italian general studied the face of Reims, who was the senior of the four officers. The calculated refusal of the cigarette had stung him, but he had neither the inclination nor the energy to lose his temper. His hatred was too deep for that.

Reims had eyes like a bird of prey, set close together, and he seemed to have to turn his head in order to change the direction of their constant gaze, which was endlessly, dangerously forward. He blinked only rarely, but when he did his lids fell and rose again mechanically, like a time exposure on a camera. There was a deep fold on the bridge of his nose, as though heavy glasses had once become embedded there and it had entailed surgery to remove them. His lips were a perfect, high-precision fit, with little incisions running across them, a fading wound from which the stitches had not yet been removed. The nostrils were large and flared, and quivered with irritation as some small nerve under one eye beat an endless tattoo somewhere near his cheekbone.

The way his hair grew seemed essentially foreign to the Italian. It stood up sharply and whirled around a double crown, where a tuft of longer hair sprouted aimlessly, forever unkempt and strangely defenceless. The colour was grey of the kind that must have been fair once, and the skin of the face, brown and leathery, changing to an obscene white on the lower neck, which looked not so much shaved as plucked, a dead chicken.

Deliberately, General Capognoni blew the scented smoke from his cigarette in the direction of Reims, saw it spiral around the aggravating head of the desiccated warlord, and noted with small pleasure the increase in the twitching as the odour of the Turkish tobacco was drawn into those huge, flared nostrils.

'Suicide is the ultimate form of cowardice,' General Egon Freiherr Von Augenstrahl suddenly declared.

'It is the height, the acme of honour,' General Reims shouted feebly.

'By killing yourself, you are doing the work of the enemy. You are wasting a bullet which should be used in battle.'

'Our orders specifically forbid us to fall into enemy hands,' Reims snapped.

'Our orders were given us by a crackpot Austrian corporal in Berlin. As a German officer, I no longer consider myself bound by orders which have allowed our tragic situation to develop.'

Kowalka laughed. 'Not a word against the Austrians,' he said lightly, 'our friend in Berlin was a corporal in the German Army. Had he stayed at home, he would have remained a private.'

There was no argument.

Capognoni studied Von Augenstrahl. A good face, young but with an undercurrent of unpleasant and disconcerting hysteria. He was tall and thin, dark for a German. There was a chain around his neck. It may have been an identity disc, but he was probably a Catholic. His mouth was disfigured by a permanent scowl, which was too dramatic not to be the expression of a weak man in search of strength. His sudden outbursts, his categorical decisions, were those of one who is reckless in attack and stubborn in defence but who is unsure of any qualities which lie beneath the surface; a man whom generals believe has it in him to be a born leader because he learns the obvious lessons too well.

'D'you know the one about Count Bobby and the Jewish stockbroker?' said Kowalka.

'Spare us your jokes,' Reims answered.

'I beg your pardon. I forgot that jokes were rationed too.'

Capognoni glanced at Kowalka, who lifted what was left of his cigarette into the air as both a salute and a toast to the generous donor. Capognoni smiled slightly, because he was polite by nature. Kowalka was a professional Austrian, and as such annoyed the Italian. He took strength, and indeed joy, in all the most flagrant vices of his race, which was insupportable for an Italian who was working hard to do just the opposite. And yet, it was only a manner of speaking, this dogged facetiousness. In action, Kowalka had proved himself not only courageous but, what is even rarer, imaginative.

His small dark eyes darted hither and thither, thinking of something to say, something amusing, at least ironic. His mouth was full of gold teeth, gold and a little white, Austrian baroque. On his upper lip lay a small moustache, not the postage stamp cultivated by Hitler, but a delicate pagoda roof. His nose was amusingly long and pointed, but split at the end like a baby's bottom. A good husband, Capognoni thought, for a wife who likes laughter and is not too vigilant.

Capognoni started thinking about women, the women of men such as these. He threw down his cigarette and stared at Reims. The Frau Gemahlin was probably one of those gaunt Teutonic creatures with a plummy, apologetic voice, too tall to be really feminine, too thin also. He imagined her pink skin, punctuated by long fair hair, like rushes, and he shuddered. When Reims had gone, she would fit admirably into black trappings, receive her condolences with the bleak affectations of suppressed heroism, and bend, a folding ruler, to place the sad flowers on the tomb. Von Augenstrahl, he guessed, had no wife. Nor, if he survived, would he ever have one. There was some obvious agony of the spirit behind the aristocratic façade, some great passion which had found no direction. He was of the stuff of martyrs, of monks, of proud, rigorous solitudes, but also of surrender to vice, to dissipation, to corruption and perversion. Temptation could never be far away with an eye so febrile and a scowl so desperate. His family was perhaps too old, the marriages had been too good for too long, the code of behaviour too elevated to be practical in an age which had no patience with chivalry.

Capognoni glanced at his watch, which had a gold case. Instead of flicking it aside to tell the time, he looked at himself. Time had no meaning any more, but he had. He saw one hazel eye, distorted by the scratches on the gold; one eye, an eyebrow, a little of an aquiline nose.

'How different,' he thought, 'am I from these uncertain Northern savages.' He was convinced that neuroses emanated from the North. His life had held no problems of the kind which would induce twitches or stammering. Mediterranean existence was as clear and as limpid as the Southern sky. There was emotion, of course, and easy tears, but they were definite medicinal advantages. Sorrow did not linger inexpressibly, to fester into complexes. If there was grief, it was immediate and very loud. Others would help by weeping just because they saw tears flowing. It needed no precise, logical reason. It cleared the mind and was good for the appetite.

He was further from home than any of them, further from the cypresses and the olives, the smell of the herbs drenched by the sun, the languid sea; further from home and the children, the yelling streets, the screeching tyres, the arguments conducted from pavement to pavement, the lizards on the sand that must have been old when the Romans were alive. He thought of his children more than of his wife. Aldo and Teresa, in their identical costumes, rear-admirals in the Italian Navy. He thought of Poppea, the white sheep-dog, a blind rug hobbling about the patio in search of shade. Yes, he thought of his wife, Donna Marcella, with her resigned, patient face, her ample bosom, her smile of dull but touching understanding. He wanted to cry, but he couldn't because of the presence of those damned Germans. They would misunderstand, as they had always misunderstood. This was a time for militant thoughts.

He remembered his pleasures, the recklessness with which he drove his red Alfa-Romeo to impress his mistresses. Ninety miles an hour in a built-up area was nothing strange, and in any case, he had an amiable relationship with the police. Amalia Portanello had been his favourite, a tall, cool blonde who might have sat for Signorelli, even for Botticelli. The smell of her perfume had lingered around the car even when she was absent. They liked to bathe at night, naked, at Fregenae.

Giovanna Petricoli had been more passionate, perhaps, but consequently more of a nuisance, since she had been impractical enough to yearn for a permanent liaison, a kind of second marriage on the side. Chiara Dossi was an actress. More sophisticated, but she had made him jealous by her unwillingness to commit herself, by her sidelong glances at door and window, by her mysterious telephone conversations with other people in his presence. Anna Maria Lisone was the wife of his best friend, which gave a subtle spice and melodrama to their acts of love. Ah, life had been full and voluptuous. What was he doing here, in the midst of a Russian winter, freezing to death? His connections could have kept him at home, at some desk job in the Ministry of War. Why was he scarcely able to move his feet, he, who loved nothing better than a bed of pine needles to walk on, and hot sand leading to the sea?

He was convinced that Italy was a warlike nation and that the temptations of her landscape and her climate must be resisted at all costs. The Romans loved life, he used to argue, and they denied themselves none of the pleasures of the body, but when the time came they marched in disciplined ranks into the frozen north, to conquer and to rule.

He suddenly imagined Reims in a bearskin, staring not at his unpromising destiny but at a foul-smelling pot of gruel, the fruit of a day's primitive hunting. Himself he saw as a Roman, all gilt and glory, ministering to the shivering savage, explaining that there is no power on earth to stop the inexorable advance of the legions.

Just then Kowalka broke the mood. 'Hey, *Generale*,' he said, 'we fought the only civilized wars, didn't we? The Austrians and the Italians. At Caporetto you ran away, at Vittorio Veneto it was our turn. It was all done as gentlemen should do it. At the first sign of an advance, the other side retreated. There was none of this nonsense of both sides trying to advance at the same time.'

Capognoni flushed under this insult. 'I don't agree,' he said stiffly. 'Wars are to be won, and every effort should be made to win them.'

Reims grunted.

'You may have complaints to register about our soldiers,' Capognoni went on with quiet fury, 'but they pale beside our complaints of German generalship.'

Reims turned on him. 'How do you allow yourself such impertinence!' he cried, the white of his eyes isolating his light blue irises from the eyelids. 'It is well known that Italian strategy leads in only one direction, backwards!'

Before Capognoni could reply, Von Augenstrahl intervened. 'What you say is unfair, Herr General, and beneath the dignity of a German officer.'

'How dare you tell me about the dignity of a German officer. I am the senior general present!' His outburst finished hoarsely as his energy ran out.

'This is our war. We cannot expect Italians, Romanians, and Hungarians to fight our war as they would fight their own.'

'Our war is their war. We are accomplishing our historic mission of saving Europe from the Mongolians, the Asiatics. It is Germany's destiny to accomplish this solemn duty of leadership. Look at the Russian prisoners, small, inferior men with slanting eyes and yellow skin, and you will understand that this war is Europe's war.'

'Were you referring to the Japanese, Herr General?' asked Kowalka.

'I was referring to the Russians, the Russian prisoners!'

'It's so long since I've seen a Russian prisoner,' said Kowalka with a humorous sigh.

'Time is up.' General Reims slowly drew his revolver and placed it on a packing-case which was serving as a table. He looked at the two other German officers and said, 'In my estimation, as senior officer present, the moment for a vital and tragic decision has arrived.'

Even in despair the Germans find the most complicated, overblown phrases, thought Capognoni.

'I made up my mind that if no relief had arrived by twelve o'clock, midday, then it would be our duty to resign ourselves to the inevitable and to obey the directive given to all officers, which is not on any account to fall into enemy hands alive. To ensure this, I order you all, with the exception of General Capognoni, over whose fate I do not presume or wish to have any jurisdiction, to take your own lives in an honourable way. Are there any questions?'

There was a moment of silence. Von Augenstrahl blinked rapidly once or twice and then said, 'Herr General, my point of view is already well known to you. I will not waste my breath reiterating. Quite apart from certain religious scruples, which I will not discuss with those who are unqualified in such matters, I regard suicide as cowardly, unsoldierly, and ungentlemanly.'

'Am I to understand that you, a German officer, refuse to obey orders?' croaked Reims.

'I cannot obey orders which are against the dictates of my conscience and of common sense,' Von Augenstrahl snapped, the perspiration running down his forehead in spite of the cold.

'You are under arrest!'

Capognoni wanted to laugh. Kowalka did. Was there no end to absurdity?

'I am leaving,' said Kowalka suddenly.

'Where to?' asked Reims. There was almost a trace of hope in his voice, as though he believed Kowalka might have some secret information which he had been withholding.

'That is a good question,' replied Kowalka. 'I wish the answer were as good. I don't know. I am going to find the Russians if I can.'

'What for?' Reims demanded.

'In order to surrender,' said Kowalka simply.

Reims's face became purple as the blood rushed wildly beneath the skin. 'Can't you leave the dirty work to our allies?' he cried.

Capognoni bit his lip. 'Yes,' he said with a composure which was surprising even to himself, 'leave the dirty work to your allies. It is in the great tradition of the German Army. It worked well in Africa; why shouldn't it work well here?'

Reims brought his fist down on the packing-case but

could find no words, since the violence of his emotions was evidently causing him some physical distress.

'Are you coming with me?' Kowalka asked Von Augen-strahl.

'No. I have two bullets left. Neither of them will be for me. They will both be for Russians.'

'One is madder than the other,' observed Kowalka. 'General Capognoni?'

'I am staying here,' said Capognoni. 'As a Roman, it amuses me to see how the barbarians prepare for the end.'

'I had no idea that a Roman would wish to emulate the barbarians in those sordid matters. Rome's greatness was that she always knew when she was beaten. She knew how to compromise. Even today she is referred to as Eternal.'

'It was always Rome's duty to set an example.'

The twitching on Reims's face increased perilously, like the end of a film beginning to run off the spool. Death was a solemn occasion, and these impertinences were desecrating it. A man only dies once. It should be done in style, with due regard for heroic self-pity and with silence for massive and lugubrious thoughts.

Kowalka dug in his tattered pocket and produced a small compass.

'East is in that direction,' he said, pointing to the un-promising horizon. 'I am going due east, towards Stalin-grad. Perhaps, with the help of the Russians, I will succeed where the entire Sixth Army failed.'

'Coward,' said Reims, whose trembling hand was attempting to slip a bullet into the chamber of his revolver.

'Coward?' answered Kowalka pleasantly. 'Perhaps.'

He tore the decorations off his uniform and lobbed them over towards Reims. 'There, does that make you feel better, Herr General?' he asked and added, 'It makes me feel better. There goes half my guilt.' He smiled disarmingly at Von Augenstrahl. 'I trust you will go in the other direction.

I have no wish to become a victim of your devotion to duty.'

'I am going west,' snapped Von Augenstrahl.

'I am delighted to hear it. General Capognoni, I hope to see you after this idiocy is over. The Hotel Imperiale at Cortina d'Ampezzo is one of my favourites. Do you ever go there?'

Capognoni did not answer.

Kowalka clicked his heels in the Prussian manner, brought his hand up in the Nazi salute, shouted, 'Heil Mozart!' and staggered out into the snow.

Von Augenstrahl gazed at Reims. 'Is there anything you wish me to . . . to tell anyone . . . if I should be lucky?'

Reims looked up gratefully, pathetically. 'My wife can look after herself,' he said gravely, 'and my sons were brought up to be officers and gentlemen. I have no fear that they will disgrace our name. Tell them I have died as they would have wished and that it had to be.'

'Heil Wagner,' murmured Capognoni, but neither of the Germans heard him.

'Tell them to destroy my dog.'

Capognoni looked at Von Augenstrahl in sudden horror, but Von Augenstrahl just nodded stiffly, his eyes shut.

This was too much to tolerate. Such was Reims's taste for suicidal heroics that he even wished a poor, healthy dog to accompany him to the kennels of Valhalla.

'Why kill an innocent dog?' he cried in spite of himself. Reims ignored him but gazed at Von Augenstrahl with baleful eyes. 'Freiherr Von Augenstrahl, we have disagreed on many points,' he said, 'but we are both German officers. I should like to shake you by the hand before I do my duty.'

Impulsively Von Augenstrahl extended his gloved hand, which Reims took in both of his, practically petrified in their tattered mittens. They looked deep into each other's eyes, like lovers, and Capognoni knew that he had never seen anything so ugly in his life. Tears suddenly spurted uncontrollably from Von Augenstrahl's dark eyes, and the whole of Reims's jaw was shuddering violently.

Almost fiercely Von Augenstrahl withdrew his hand from the moribund grasp of the older man, saluted in the traditional pre-Nazi manner, turned, and walked out of the hut.

Capognoni felt an expression on his face which he had never experienced before, an expression which was probably one of revulsion, the anguish of a man with humanism in his blood faced by inhumanity. He glanced at Reims.

Reims, with much groaning and grunting, began to struggle out of his greatcoat. Instinctively Capognoni wished to help him, but restrained himself. He did not want to be party to this odious rite about which he understood nothing, nor did he feel qualified to interfere with the exquisite pleasures of a man who tasted every whiff of absurdity as though it were a rare vintage of human experience.

The revolver was in readiness. Reims searched his satchel with fingers that could hardly obey him any more, fingers as puzzled as those of a child when they find an unknown texture, as lost as those of a young monkey at grips with an unpeeled banana. At last he drew out a couple of medals and began to pin them to his tunic. He was in no condition to do this, and one after the other, they fell to the ground, but he did not notice. Then he shut his eyes and passed his hand over his breast with an almost feminine gesture. His eyes opened again when he realized that the medals were not there. He looked down and began to whimper. Like a baby whose toy has fallen out of its pen, he reached for the floor with no conviction of being able to reach them. Appealingly, he looked at Capognoni. The whimpering too was that of a baby, or of a dog locked out.

Capognoni returned the look steadily. 'Bastard,' he thought, 'to condemn your dog to death.'

Still the whimpering went on.

Capognoni felt like drawing his own pistol, putting a couple of bullets into Reims, and spoiling the whole elaborate ritual, but he did not move. It was crueller to wait.

Then Reims frowned, passed his hand over his heart again, let it loiter over the ribbons, and looked straight forward. He cleared his throat as though he were going to shout and then began singing the national anthem in the high, unsteady voice of an aged woman.

Suddenly Capognoni's taste was mortally offended and, without pausing to think, he sang *Vesti la Guiba* in a penetrating tenor, filling the air with sarcastic sobs as the third-rate artists do in Neapolitan restaurants.

In the middle of a phrase, Capognoni stopped. Reims could no longer hear him. The veins on his temple were standing out like flexed muscles, and the blood was racing around on the last lap of the race. Reims seemed transparent, a mere network of arteries exposed by the dissolving flesh. There was a report, and he fell to the floor motionless, the bitter draught from the ill-fitting door agitating the little tuft of defenceless hair on top of his head as the wind will play with a tuft of grass.

For a moment Capognoni was stunned as the noise of the explosion seemed to inhabit the room, dying more slowly than Reims, and then he began to retch, but as his stomach was empty it produced no more than an agonizing pain and watering eyes. When he recovered his composure, he reflected how pleasant it was to be alone, to be unobserved. Surely a man could stand anything when there was no need to keep up appearances. He looked at the room as though he were seeing it for the first time. The rough beams had a sort of beauty. It was like being ill and alone, when the eye, for want of the indiscriminate everyday excitements, began to find an elusive symmetry in damp patches on the ceiling or could study the patterns of raindrops on a window and find a rarefied satisfaction in watching their antics. The silence had the sound of music. The air was cold, but he consciously took a deep breath and noticed how clean it was, sterile as alcohol, white and simple. He thought of nothing and took pleasure in the thought.

Such pleasures do not last forever. They come only as reactions to some desperate involvement, and soon he began to remember how cruel the cold really was. As he huddled in his corner, he tried to keep his eyes from straying towards Reims, but the very fact of this conscious avoidance seemed to swell the presence of that stupid corpse, so grotesquely sprawled in the slush.

He tried to think of pleasant things, as he had done before, when the others were still in the hut. It should be easier to think of Italy now. After all, he was alone. He thought of Capri, but all he saw in his mind's eye was a post-card. The sea was too blue to be true, the houses too pink. In a silent, intimate panic, he realized that too much had happened for him to think pleasantly. It was like dropping off to sleep with the determination to have sweet dreams. No sooner does sleep come than they turn to nightmares. Better to have no thoughts. It was too cold not to think, and there was that mess on the floor. He listened for the sound of the explosion and could not be sure that it had died away yet.

Grimly he opened the door to the thoughts which were crowding in on him and from which there was evidently no escape, no relief. A wretched dog sentenced to death for no other reason than that the lachrymose vanity of a man demanded a funeral pyre large enough to emphasize his station. Perhaps Reims would never have indulged in all the nauseous pomposity if there had been no witnesses. If he had been alone, he probably would never even have killed himself. No actor can give of his best in an empty theatre. No use dying if you don't haunt some memory or other, if you don't leave an aftertaste.

Capognoni thought of himself. His troops had not fought well, nor had he. His temperament was too volatile for battles of attrition, especially when reason declared them to be lost from the outset. How could he have demanded of his men to attack with the bayonet simply for the privilege of delaying an inevitable retreat, simply in order to drag out a preordained disaster? It was surely no proof of courage voluntarily to disobey your own intelligence. Driving a racing car at 150 miles an hour, that is courage linked to intelligence. But there again, there is a public gallery to play to. An error of judgment at that speed, and you go to your death observed, applauded, regretted, heroic. Not as in all this snow, neglected, unidentified.

He had seen the Germans seize the ascendancy in motor racing, backed up by huge government subsidies which had financed machinery of unparalleled brutality. The drivers sat at the wheels of those monstrous weapons and forced them around the tracks ferociously, insensitively. The Italians kept up by sheer artistry, by coaxing and cajoling their slower cars into prodigious performances, by talking to their engines, by whispering to the blistered tyres, by humanizing the inanimate.

That was courage! Italian history was peppered with redoubtable *condottieri*, exquisite murderers, incredible heroes, and, more recently, daredevils by the dozen in the riskiest of sports. Any fool can be courageous in pitched battle if he is stupid enough and if his indoctrination has divorced him from all contact with the human race, but it takes real courage to be burned like Savonarola, with the clear realization of your sacrifice, and with your intelligence untrammelled to the end. But then, Savonarola too was burned in public. He died before witnesses. The aftertaste was there to take over from the flames.

How dismal to starve to death. What if the Russians never came? Capognoni began looking for something to write on, some message he could leave. Then he remembered that he had lost his pen and that his pen, even before he lost it, had had no ink in it. There was a complicated finality to this conspiracy to wipe him off the face of the globe anonymously. He began to be convinced that he would starve. He listened and heard nothing. He shouted and was surprised to hear his own voice.

If the Russians did come, what would he do? Surrender, of course. It was logical. There would be no witnesses except a few Russians, and it was all they would expect. Then he glanced at Reims and felt some of the old resentment welling up within him. He remembered the taunts from that paltry Lohengrin and the beady looks of complicity from Kowalka with his cynical nonsense about Caporetto and Vittorio Veneto, of war fought as a tinselled minuet between civilized nations. He had abrupt visions of Africa, of Italy's place in the sun, and of the cruel complex which had endlessly turned the most glorious dreams into embarrassing realities. He thought of the roads which had been built in Ethiopia, only, as it happened, to facilitate the British advance. What was wrong?

He was wrong. He had thought of surrender. Not only had he thought of surrender, but he had thought of surrender as logical. He was wrong, and he was Italy. Long enough had he absorbed insults by pretending not to have heard them, long enough had he been polite, compliant, diplomatic. To win, it was not sufficient to wait for the enemy to move and then to react. To win, it was imperative to dare, to grasp the initiative. He should have seized

Kowalka by the throat at the time of that affront instead of sitting back and relying on sarcasm. He should have shouted Reims down, shot him, anything. His natural politeness would always be taken for weakness by these caricatures of men. Now he wanted them all back, alive; he wished to play the scene over again. He was furious.

Two shots rang out. Von Augenstrahl? A decision, quickly. He used to hate going to the dentist, because he invariably reacted to the pain of the drill before the instrument had begun its work. One day he had relaxed completely and forced himself to believe that his visit to the dentist was a daily occurrence, of no particular note. Although the drill hurt abominably, the operation was over before he allowed himself to be impressed by it and he had emerged into the street a man of resolution. Danger was a thing to be drifted into, not a thing to make elaborate preparations for. Allow your thoughts to wander.

A voice called out in the distance. Two voices. Capognoni glanced at the beams and reflected on the complexity of wood. What a fuss to make. Singing the national anthem and pinning on those bits of tin, sent out by the thousands in order to boost morale. Quickly he studied the wood again and then lit a cigarette. His hand was shaking, but only slightly. He presumed it was the cold.

Slowly the door opened and a sub-machine gun edged shyly into the hut. It was followed by a young Russian soldier, padded against the cold so that he looked almost like a diver. Only his face showed, a pug-nosed, spotty, adolescent face with big blue terrified eyes. His mouth was open, and the breath flowed from it like a caption balloon in a cartoon.

"*Raus*," said the Russian nervously.

Capognoni smiled and answered in Italian that he was more comfortable where he was.

''*Raus?*' said the Russian once again, inflecting the word as though it were a question.

Capognoni answered again in Italian, and the Russian, after a moment's hesitation, stumbled out and called for someone with more authority.

Capognoni inhaled his cigarette with relish and read the word *Nazionale* printed on it over and over again.

A lieutenant entered and said, '*Sprechen Sie Deutsch?*'

'*Lei parla Italiano?*' asked Capognoni.

''*Raus,*' shouted the lieutenant, who seemed to be in a hurry.

'*Parlez-vous français?*' said Capognoni.

The lieutenant advanced towards him, stumbling over Reims. Capognoni held up a restraining hand.

Annoyed, the lieutenant snapped, '*Sie sind Kriegsgefangener.' Raus.*'

There seemed to be nothing for it. The only means of communication was that damned language which had plagued him ever since he had come to Russia.

'I refuse to surrender,' said Capognoni in German, quite quietly. The lieutenant did not appear to understand.

'We are still at war,' Capognoni added.

The lieutenant smiled quite pleasantly. 'What do you want to do about it?' he asked.

Capognoni smiled in return. He was acting a scene which was worthy of him, and he knew the value of each nuance. Slowly he opened his holster and as slowly drew his pistol.

The lieutenant's amiable, cheeky smile faded from his face as he suddenly became conscious of an unbelievable peril. He reached for his own gun and fumbled with it. Capognoni aimed his pistol slowly and deliberately at the lieutenant, but did not fire. It was the lieutenant who eventually fired, and Capognoni sat quite still.

'You tell them . . .' he said with difficulty, 'that the Italian Army . . . was the last to cease resistance on this front.'

The lieutenant was angry. 'Who the hell cares,' he cried, 'so long as we're winning?'

Capognoni looked at his audience and knew from the troubled expression on the lieutenant's face that his gesture would live on ineradicably in at least one mind. The aftertaste.

In a fury, the lieutenant brought his fist crashing on to the packing-case and howled, 'What did you do that for?'

Capognoni opened his mouth to reply, but died instead.

'Crackpot,' said the lieutenant, who was a conscript and engaged to be married.

**Bestselling British Fiction in Panther Books**

**Bestselling Transatlantic Fiction in Panther Books**

| | | | |
|---|---|---|---|
| THE SOT-WEED FACTOR | John Barth | £1.50 | ☐ |
| BEAUTIFUL LOSERS | Leonard Cohen | 60p | ☐ |
| THE FAVOURITE GAME | Leonard Cohen | 40p | ☐ |
| TARANTULA | Bob Dylan | 50p | ☐ |
| DESOLATION ANGELS | Jack Kerouac | 50p | ☐ |
| THE DHARMA BUMS | Jack Kerouac | 40p | ☐ |
| BARBARY SHORE | Norman Mailer | 40p | ☐ |
| AN AMERICAN DREAM | Norman Mailer | 40p | ☐ |
| THE NAKED AND THE DEAD | Norman Mailer | 60p | ☐ |
| THE BRAMBLE BUSH | Charles Mergendahl | 40p | ☐ |
| TEN NORTH FREDERICK | John O'Hara | 50p | ☐ |
| FROM THE TERRACE | John O'Hara | 75p | ☐ |
| OURSELVES TO KNOW | John O'Hara | 60p | ☐ |
| THE DICE MAN | Luke Rhinehart | 95p | ☐ |
| COCKSURE | Mordecai Richler | 60p | ☐ |
| ST URBAIN'S HORSEMAN | Mordecai Richler | 50p | ☐ |
| THE CITY AND THE PILLAR | Gore Vidal | 40p | ☐ |
| BLUE MOVIE | Terry Southern | 60p | ☐ |
| BREAKFAST OF CHAMPIONS | Kurt Vonnegut Jr | 50p | ☐ |
| SLAUGHTERHOUSE 5 | Kurt Vonnegut Jr | 50p | ☐ |
| MOTHER NIGHT | Kurt Vonnegut Jr | 40p | ☐ |
| PLAYER PIANO | Kurt Vonnegut Jr | 50p | ☐ |
| GOD BLESS YOU, MR ROSEWATER | Kurt Vonnegut Jr | 50p | ☐ |
| WELCOME TO THE MONKEY HOUSE | Kurt Vonnegut Jr | 75p | ☐ |

*All these books are available at your local bookshop or newsagent, or can be ordered direct from the publisher. Just tick the titles you want and fill in the form below.*

Name .........................................................................................................

Address ....................................................................................................

.................................................................................................................

Write to Panther Cash Sales, PO Box 11, Falmouth, Cornwall TR10 9EN.

Please enclose remittance to the value of the cover price plus:

UK: 18p for the first book plus 8p per copy for each additional book ordered to a maximum charge of 66p.

BFPO and EIRE: 18p for the first book plus 8p per copy for the next 6 books, thereafter 3p per book.

OVERSEAS: 20p for the first book and 10p for each additional book.

*Granada Publishing reserve the right to show new retail prices on covers, which may differ from those previously advertised in the text or elsewhere.*